TUXEDO PARK

TUXEDO PARK

Basil Copper

CHIVERS
THORNDIKE

This Large Print edition is published by BBC Audiobooks Ltd, Bath, England and by Thorndike Press®, Waterville, Maine, USA.

Published in 2004 in the U.K. by arrangement with the author.

Published in 2004 in the U.S. by arrangement with Basil Copper.

U.K. Hardcover ISBN 0–7540–7791–8 (Chivers Large Print)
U.K. Softcover   ISBN 0–7540–7792–6 (Camden Large Print)
U.S. Softcover   ISBN 0–7862–6377–6 (Nightingale)

The text of this Large Print edition is unabridged.
Other aspects of the book may vary from the original edition.

Set in 16 pt. New Times Roman.

Printed in Great Britain on acid-free paper.

British Library Cataloguing in Publication Data available

Library of Congress Cataloging-in-Publication Data

Copper, Basil.
   Tuxedo park / Basil Copper.
       p.   cm.
   ISBN 0–7862–6377–6 (lg. print : sc : alk. paper)
   1. Faraday, Mike (Fictitious character)—Fiction. 2. Private investigators—California—Los Angeles—Fiction. 3. Los Angeles (Calif.)—Fiction. 4. Children of the rich—Fiction.
5. Bodyguards—Fiction. 6. Large type books. I. Title.
PR6053.O658T89 2004
823'.914—dc22   2003071120

CHAPTER ONE

1

A jet aircraft made a pure white scimitar-slash on the eye-searing expanse of the sky as I got out my five-year-old powder-blue Buick and slammed the driving door, the sun hot and heavy on my head. The man in the glassed-in booth at the entrance gate to the private estate nodded affably as though it was a pretty chilly afternoon. He actually had the door of the booth closed and not a bead of perspiration showed on the dome of his Yul Brynner-style haircut.

'Good afternoon.'

The voice was low and polite but I noticed the heavy pistol he was wearing at his waist. There was also a fairly powerful shotgun suspended from clips on the far wall of his cubby-hole so I didn't put too much stock on his gentility. I guessed that was maybe why he kept the door closed. The glass looked to be bullet-proof come to that.

'My name's Faraday,' I said. 'I have an appointment for half-past two with Mrs Van Gimpel.'

'Oh, yes.'

He nodded and ran his finger down a heavy leather-covered appointments book on the desk in front of him.

'If you'll just wait a moment.'

I went and admired the scenery while he dialled a number on a gun-metal grey telephone. The booth was set in the left-hand wing of the massive wrought-iron gates that looked like something left over from Louis' place at Versailles; beneath the deep shade of an overhanging spread of chestnuts. I set fire to a cigarette and enjoyed the breeze that was blowing up on the bluff here.

Way down to the left the forest fell steeply, ending in cliffs and gorges while beyond the fringe of foliage the Pacific rolled, blue-green in the more shallow water, a deep violet farther out. The rusty red of kelp beds floated midway between the two and a few leg of mutton sails dotted the expanse like a scarlet and white rash. It was something I'd seen thousands of times and thought nothing of yet it still brought people from all over the world; for business, for pleasure, or retirement.

The gateman was gesturing again now, so I strolled over, the faint blue cloud of my cigarette smoke whipped into trailing feathers of vapour by the wind. He had the window open, looking smart and lean in his well-cut lightweight blue uniform. I was wearing my best grey suit today with a rather becoming polka-dot tie but I could see the disapproval in back of his eyes at the scuffed condition of the toe-caps on my size nines.

'Mrs Van Gimpel is expecting you, Mr Faraday,' he said as though I might have doubts about it. He swivelled in his box, pointed down the shadowy drive that led from the entrance gates.

'Spanish Oaks is the fourth estate down on the left. It's about a two-mile drive on the private road but you can't miss it.'

I thanked him and walked back over to where I'd left the Buick. The metal was simmering nicely now and I could feel the heat searing into my shoulder-blades through my suit even before I sat down. The gateman must have pressed a button because one half the big gate slid back with a barely audible rumble, controlled electronically from the cubicle.

I gave the gateman a wave as I went by but he was already answering the phone, completely oblivious to me. Probably somebody wanted some lace doilies delivered. I saw the gate shutting smoothly behind me in the rear-mirror. My smile lasted me almost all the way to Mrs Van Gimpel's place.

The road went on straight and smooth beneath the cool, dappled green twilight of the woods with now and again cross-roads with white-painted noticeboards and, sometimes, vast tarmac clearings cut in the forest; and I glimpsed silent estates shimmering beneath the sunlight; well-shaved lawns and once, above the flowering hedges, something that looked like a French château with domes,

3

cupolas and a green-tiled roof.

I looked for Louis and his coach with six white horses but there were only two tall blondes, their long hair tied back, exercising horses on the well-kept road surface. They drew rein to let me pass, giving me chintzy looks with their well-bred eyes. I didn't know whether eyes could be well-bred or not, but it gave me something to occupy my mind this afternoon.

Stella had said Mrs Van Gimpel had sounded worried when she'd had her secretary phone. She'd come on herself after Stella had told the secretary I was out and had emphasised the urgency of our meeting. Whatever was burning her I smelt money and hadn't wasted any time in dragging my under-wear over here.

The estates drifted by in a shimmer of early afternoon sun and I was becoming somewhat soporific with the atmosphere out here. I always get like that when I'm brought in contact with the moneyed classes. Which isn't often as I usually operate at the gritty end of the P.I. business; the sort where one ends up beaten silly and dumped in a trash-can in some alley. That's looking on the bright side, of course. Sometimes one can get in serious trouble.

I jolted awake as something like a sugar-cake started composing itself from the golden haze above the tree-tops fringing the private road. There were plenty of Spanish oaks about; plantations of them, so I didn't need the elaborate wrought iron sign that was hanging on chains above the entrance pillars; there was even Spanish moss dangling from the trees. I looked for Ashley Wilkes too but it was probably his afternoon off.

The Courtenay Estates had been built about sixty years ago for the well-heeled and those living on tax-free, inflation-proof millionaires' pensions. Certain people in L.A. called it Tuxedo Park. I knew what they meant, of course. But this was the first time I'd been up here. I was about to find out.

2

I drove in under the big sign and drifted down a serpentine drive, winding in and out between the oaks, the wedding-cake house gradually rising before me. Two Filipino gardeners were tending the velvet lawns and they had the sprinklers going everywhere. I pulled the Buick in near a marble fountain that was playing in a red gravel concourse and got out, the sun hot and hard on my back.

There was a garage block farther down, built into a stone bluff below the level of the house; I could see a dark green Rolls-Royce, a scarlet Mercedes and a white Porsche. After that I stopped counting. I went up a flight of steps that evidently led to the house above, feeling like a second class citizen. All the while the house was growing before me.

At first I had mentally compared it to Fontainebleau. Now that I could see it properly the correct analogy would have been Ludwig, the mad King of Bavaria. I guessed some eccentric millionaire of the twenties had built it. No-one could have stood the cost today. And few people, even in California, could have afforded to run it. I mentally upped my rates.

I could hear music now and splashing. I came out from behind a flowering hedge into full sunlight. There was a serpentine swim pool that seemed to go on for ever, filled with cool-looking green water, set in the well-shaved turf; and a marble tiled surround that was decked out with blue umbrellas and cane chairs.

That wasn't all. There was a colour TV set on one of the tables with the images flickering away to itself with the sound turned off. The music was coming from a tape machine that was standing on the next table down. It looked like the consumer society gone mad to me. But who was I to complain. There was a girl in the pool, swimming down one of the esses that led up to where I was standing on the marble paving.

She was quite something. She wore nothing but a small pair of white briefs and her tanned body undulated as she went into a crawl, her clouds of blonde hair floating out behind her. She had a beautiful but sullen face and her expression was insolent as she spotted me standing there. Her breasts were insolent too, if one could describe them so. I could and did.

She trod water, staring at me like someone was burning linoleum under her nostrils, pushing away the strands of wet hair from her face with her right hand.

'You might throw me that robe,' she said.

'I might,' I said. 'But the view's fine without.' She looked at me with smouldering green eyes. 'Quit the joking. It's cold in here.'

I crossed over to one of the cane chairs and gave her the robe like she said. She held it over her head with one hand and cruised to the far side of the pool, running agilely up the wooden ladder and putting the white towelling robe on, keeping her back turned to me. The modesty seemed a little late. She was walking around the pool now. She was a lot taller than I figured and her sensational legs were occasionally in view through the gap in the robe.

She slumped down into one of the chairs in front of me, crossing her tanned legs and reached for a pack of cigarettes and a silver lighter on the table top.

'You know you're trespassing.'

I shook my head.

'I think not. Mrs Van Gimpel asked me out

7

here.'

She pouted. It didn't do anything for her. 'Oh, mother. So you're one of those.'

'I don't know what you mean,' I said. 'My name's Faraday.'

She raised her eyebrows.

'I'm Valerie Van Gimpel, if it's any business of yours.'

'It isn't,' I said. 'You look like a Valerie.'

She ignored that, lighting the cigarette, puffing out a cloud of blue smoke, studying me under lowered lids.

'What do you do, Mr Faraday?'

'I'm a private detective,' I said. 'It's no secret. What do you do?'

The girl's face had subtly changed now.

'Well, well,' she said. 'I'm a private citizen.' I grinned, looking round at the ritzy set-up. 'It must occupy a lot of your time,' I said. The girl in the white towelling robe shrugged. 'It does, Mr Faraday.'

Before we could go any further there came a thudding noise on the turf and a horse and rider sailed over the high flowering hedge separating the pool area from the grounds. A tall girl with blonde hair tied back drew the big black mare up with a clittering of hooves and slid down from the saddle. She ignored us and went down to tie the horse to one of the sunshade uprights.

'You should sell tickets,' I said.

The girl smiled faintly.

8

'It's only Erica,' she said. 'My sister. Showing off as usual.'

I recognised the girl on the horse then as one of the two I'd passed on the road on my way in. If Valerie Van Gimpel was arrogant Erica was so classy she didn't even acknowledge her sister, but I could see her studying me from below her long eyelashes.

'I guess I'll go find your mother,' I said. 'The conversation here is becoming quite exhausting.'

'You'll find her up at the house, Mr Faraday,' the girl said absently. 'I wish I could say it had been nice to meet you.'

'It's been nice seeing you,' I said.

I left the two there in the odd silence and went on up the garden, the wind freshening a little now, conscious that one of the gardeners was operating a big scarlet sit-on mower in the far distance, gliding up and down to get that well-manicured look on the emerald turf.

The vast double doors in the entrance porch of Spanish Oaks were thrown back and beyond I could see an enormous hall floored in black and white marble across which rays of sun shot dazzling shafts to make a cathedral of the interior. Before I'd got up the steps a tall, handsome negro in his forties was standing smiling in the open doorway.

He was dressed formally in a black cutaway; pin-stripe trousers, white waistcoat, with a black bow-tie.

'Good afternoon, sir. You'll be Mr Faraday. My name is Joseph. I'm the butler.'

'Mrs Van Gimpel is expecting me,' I said.

Joseph was looking me up and down shrewdly. 'I am well aware of that, sir,' he said gravely. 'Will you come in, please.'

I walked into the dim coolness of the hall. At the same moment I was seized from behind by two immensely strong hands. Then I was cartwheeling through the air.

CHAPTER TWO

1

I landed on my back with an impact that drove the breath from me and went skidding along the tiling. But reflexes were working now. This seemed a crazy household but if they wanted to play it that way I'd give them their money's-worth. I twisted aside, avoiding a rush by Joseph, who had a set smile on his face. I caught him a tap behind the ear as he went by and it was his turn to cartwheel.

He landed against an expensive-looking cabinet in the dusky hall and spent a few seconds preventing it from crashing to the floor.

'Are you mad or what?' I said as he straightened up before rushing at me again.

'Merely orders, sir,' he said gravely.

I dropped to one knee and his fist whistled aimlessly past. I had an arm-lock on him while he was still off balance and he grunted with pain. But he was immensely strong and I had a job to hold him. He kicked back, trying to get the heel of his right foot behind my knee.

I was a little unbalanced and had to let go. He whirled quickly but I was no longer there and his clutching fingers found air. I danced away back toward the stair which wound its way upwards in a curving spiral.

'You want to tell me about this?' I said.

Joseph shook his head, perspiration gleaming in among the roots of his tightly curled hair.

'One of us is going to get hurt if this keeps up,' I said.

His teeth glinted in his smile as he came back. I had the measure of him now and I got a jab in to the body as he rushed by. He grunted with pain this time. I'd done a good deal of unarmed combat in my time with the marines but I didn't want to pull all the stops out. He seemed such a nice guy except for being crazy.

I chopped him again while he was still going away from me. This time he did a sort of fancy little dance and I knew I'd hurt him. He went up against the far wall with a crash that could have been heard clear to the swim-pool. He shook his head and came back doggedly. It

11

may have been my imagination but I fancied he looked a little grey beneath his pigmentation.

He was breathing heavily between his open teeth but he kept a sort of politeness about him that would have been comical under any other circumstances. Like he was the butler and still observing the rudiments of etiquette. His whole actions were insane to me but maybe it was a fairly normal sort of routine for this eccentric household.

I was getting tired of horsing around and I decided to stop him. Maybe I was getting a little offguard and he was flailing too much with his fists. I wasn't quite quick enough with my footwork and he got in a left to my jaw while I was still unbalanced. I felt that all right. The next thing I knew I was sliding away on my back at a smart clip. The crack as my head hit the base of a china cabinet brought a chuckle from Joseph.

'You must have a heavy bill for breakages if you treat all your guests like this,' I said.

He shook his head with an admiring smile. 'You have style, Mr Faraday.'

'So have you,' I said. 'But it's a style I can do without.'

I was on my feet again now. The big negro looked at me mockingly.

'Had enough?'

'We've only just begun,' I told him.

I dropped to one knee, easily avoiding his

12

mad rush. I got the right hold and he flew over my shoulder. He slid so far I lost sight of him in the gloom.

It was only when I heard the crash of breaking glass that I realised he'd reached the same china cabinet on the far wall.

I went over and looked down at him. He was just coming around.

'That will do, Joseph,' a woman's voice said from the stairhead above.

Joseph opened his eyes with difficulty.

'Very well, madam.'

His eyes focused on me.

'I hope I didn't hurt you too much, Mr Faraday.'

I grinned, reaching to help him up.

'I think I'll survive,' I said.

Joseph brushed himself down, still wincing with pain. But he remained dignified.

'I'd like a quiet word with you before you leave, sir.'

'Sure,' I said. 'To fix up the return match.'

I turned, looking up toward the tall, stately woman with iron-grey hair who could only be Mrs Van Gimpel. She stood leaning on a stick by the carved balustrade at the head of the stairs.

'Forgive the little test, Mr Faraday. I considered it necessary. I think you will do nicely.'

2

'Question is, whether you'll do me, Mrs Van Gimpel,' I said.

I was halfway up the stairs now. She gave a dry chuckle, waiting for me to join her on the landing.

'I was told you had a sense of humour, Mr Faraday.'

'So I have,' I said. 'One needs it around here. Your private judo classes must come out expensive over the year.'

Mrs Van Gimpel gurgled with delight. She was some woman all right. She looked down absently at the far side of the hall.

'I never liked that cabinet anyway,' she said.

I was up to her level now and could see her more clearly by the light coming in from a big round window on the landing. She looked like Florence Bates in her heyday. Which meant she was hearty, brisk and formidable. She couldn't have been much more than fifty or so and I now noticed that she leaned heavily on a silver-handled stick. She looked at me with very frank brown eyes.

'That was a first-rate work-out, Mr Faraday. Your reputation hasn't been exaggerated. We'll put that on your tab. You'll not find me ungenerous.'

She looked at me critically.

'You need a new suit, young man.'

'That was a new suit,' I said. 'Before your butler got through with it.'

She hooted again.

'We'll get along fine, Mr Faraday.'

'You are Mrs Van Gimpel?' I said. 'My secretary told me the client sounded worried. It doesn't seem like that to me.'

The grey-haired woman put her hand on my arm, looking around the broad landing like there might be spies about.

'She didn't exaggerate, Mr Faraday. Don't let my façade fool you. I'm just keeping up appearances.'

'You did fool me,' I said.

Mrs Van Gimpel led me over to a half-open doorway at the left of the stairway. It gave on to a light, airy library that looked as big as a ballroom.

'This is where I conduct all my business, Mr Faraday. We won't be disturbed here.'

She saw my glance rest on her walking cane. She bit her lip.

'I was riding up until last year, Mr Faraday. Arthritis of the hip. It struck suddenly and turned me into an old woman overnight.'

'You'll never be an old woman,' I said.

Mrs Van Gimpel shook her head.

'Kind but untrue. Please sit down near the window where I can have a good look at you.'

I sank into the 18th century leather wing chair, catching a glimpse of myself in a glass

15

bookcase opposite. I smoothed down my dishevelled hair and re-knotted my tie. Mrs Van Gimpel had gone to sit behind a green-leather top desk which came from the same century. She flushed slightly.

'Would you like to go tidy yourself up, Mr Faraday?'

'It's all right, Mrs Van Gimpel,' I said. 'If the case goes on like this it will be hardly worth it.'

She smiled faintly, pressing a button on a small console that stood on a corner of the desk.

'We'll be having some tea in a few minutes. Perhaps your feathers will feel a little less ruffled then. I can assure you that scene downstairs was arranged for a very good purpose.'

I didn't say anything, merely looked through the big bay window behind the desk which had a magnificent view of the grounds of the mansion and the distant mountains. I could see the swim-pool from here so I gathered Mrs Van Gimpel had noticed my arrival and the events following.

'You've met my daughters,' she said softly, like she'd read my thoughts.

'Briefly,' I said, keeping my eyes on the girl Valerie, who was still sitting by the pool. There was no sign of her sister, Erica. She'd probably taken the mare to the stables.

'It's about them I wanted to talk to you,' she went on.

16

She riffled around on the desk for a moment or two, her brow creased with lots of minute lines. Now that I had time to study her better I could see that she must have been a very handsome woman when younger.

Her daughters were there to prove it. She found what she was looking for after a moment, and scribbled something with a gold pen in green ink on the back of an envelope. She flung it across at me. She had a humorous expression on her face so I didn't take offence. I was even less offended when she explained.

'There's no need to open it, Mr Faraday. It contains a cheque for three thousand dollars. As you can imagine from my life-style there's plenty more where that came from. Money is absolutely no object. Let me know when you want some more.'

'I'll do that,' I said, putting the envelope in my pocket, where it seemed to burn a hole in the lining. 'You'll get a receipt and an itemised account.'

Mrs Van Gimpel leaned forward across the desk, strain for the first time appearing on her face.

'You carry a gun, Mr Faraday?'

'On occasion,' I said. 'I'm licensed for it. Why?'

There came a rapping on the door. My hostess' face was transformed.

'Ah,' she said briskly. 'Here's Joseph with the tea.'

She dropped her voice, speaking clear and low while the butler was still out of earshot.

'Because you're going to need it on this case.'

CHAPTER THREE

1

'You'll have to spell it out,' I said.

Mrs Van Gimpel shrugged.

'I'll get to it in a moment, Mr Faraday. Let us just digest our tea in peace. Regard this as a time out of war.'

I looked at Joseph reflectively. He was wincing as he poured the tea from a silver pot so I guessed he was feeling things more than I was.

'You mean to say I get another work-out with your butler after tea,' I said.

The grey-haired woman exploded with laughter and Joseph was overcome with a sudden attack of coughing. I guess he would have turned red had it been technically possible.

'I wasn't referring to that, Mr Faraday.'

Joseph gave me an even smile as he passed my teacup and a small plate of delicately cut sandwiches. I had some crack ready about the gracious life of the Deep South but discarded it as inappropriate. We ate in silence for a moment or two and Mrs Van Gimpel didn't speak again until Joseph had withdrawn.

Then she sat back at her desk and lit a Turkish cigarette which she smoked in a long holder. She smiled at my expression.

'By all means smoke also if you wish, Mr Faraday. I knew you wouldn't want one of these.'

'How did you guess?'

She shook her head, her eyes flickering down toward the still figure of her daughter by the swim-pool.

'You're not the type.'

She turned back to me, putting her firm, capable hands together on the blotter in front of her. The pungent Turkish tobacco burned with a thin blue smoke, rising slowly from the holder clenched between the fingers of her right hand.

'You've heard of the San Rosario Corporation, Mr Faraday?'

'Who hasn't,' I said. 'Perfumes, cosmetics, boutiques, high fashion.'

Mrs Van Gimpel raised her eyebrows.

'You're remarkably well-informed, Mr Faraday.'

'I'd have to be blind not to see the advertisements,' I said. 'Not to mention the products.'

'Perhaps,' the grey-haired woman said softly. 'Without putting too fine a point on it,

I'm the San Rosario Corporation.'

'Now you do surprise me,' I said.

She nodded.

'Exactly,' she said drily. 'For all intents and purposes. I have a board, of course. But I built the whole thing; I call the shots; I control the shares.'

She glared at me fiercely.

'I run it.'

I grinned.

'Fine. Who's arguing?'

Mrs Van Gimpel smiled too.

'Forgive me, Mr Faraday. I get carried away when I think what I've put into the business. It's an empire really. We have subsidiaries in twenty-three overseas countries.'

'Only twenty-three?' I said. 'And they'd have to be overseas, wouldn't they. Except for Mexico.'

Mrs Van Gimpel drew herself up, her eyebrows arched.

'Precisely, Mr Faraday. I'm not expressing myself well. I have two daughters, as you've noticed. Wild, attractive girls. I have to keep a sharp eye on them but it's difficult. I don't want them to get into the wrong hands; make bad marriages. Do you follow me?'

I shifted uncomfortably in my chair, holding out my teacup for a re-fill.

'I'm not quite sure,' I said. 'I don't do chaperone work.'

Mrs Van Gimpel paused in the tea-pouring,

20

shook her head firmly.

'I'm not talking about that, Mr Faraday. I'm talking about gun-stuff.'

2

The remark was so incongruous in such elegant surroundings that I looked at her again. But there was no doubt she was serious. I remembered the negro butler. Not that I was likely to forget him. Though I could have taken him at a pinch I had specialist knowledge. He wasn't there just for ornament. Maybe as an additional safeguard against intruders on the plush precincts of Courtenay Estates.

I went at the subject from a slightly different tangent.

'Are we talking about both girls?' I said. 'Or one in particular.'

Mrs Van Gimpel shook her head. Her eyes were wary now.

'I'm talking about Valerie specifically. She's the biggest problem. I'm not sure about Erica. She needs watching too.'

She sighed, putting her porcelain cup down with a chink in the brittle silence.

'I've been a widow for fifteen years, Mr Faraday. It becomes an intolerable burden sometimes.'

'I'm sorry,' I said. 'I can see how it would

be.'

Mrs Van Gimpel nodded, her eyes searching my face.

'Yes. I think you do understand, Mr Faraday. I'm glad I chose you.'

'I'm still not clear what you want me to do,' I said. 'You mentioned gun-stuff . . .'

The grey-haired woman made a peremptory gesture and leaned forward in her chair, her walking stick clattering unheeded to the floor.

'There's a man in L.A., Mr Faraday. He has taken far too much interest in my youngest daughter. From what I hear he has criminal connections.'

She shrugged.

'It's no use talking to Valerie. She's at an age when someone like her mother is prehistoric. You might talk to her.'

I nodded.

'I see. You want me to lean on the boy friend?'

Mrs Van Gimpel raised her eyebrows.

'You haven't heard who he is yet, Mr Faraday.'

I gave her one of my best smiles.

'He's eight feet tall, as strong as King Kong and owns half of L.A., Mrs Van Gimpel. I always get those sort of cases.'

The grey-haired woman gave another hooting laugh and sat back in her chair. She tapped ash off the cigarette in the long holder.

'I like your style, Mr Faraday. That's about

the size of it. Though it's not quite so bad and so crude as you put it.'

'I always like to put it badly and crudely,' I said. 'That way it's a pleasant surprise if it comes out better.'

Mrs Van Gimpel put her hands together on her blotter and frowned at me.

'Help yourself to sandwiches and cake, Mr Faraday. I want to choose my words carefully now.'

I did like she said and picked up her walking cane at the same time. She thanked me absently. I walked back over to my chair, taking in the gold and green tranquillity of the garden.

The girl Valerie sat on at the pool; she had on dark glasses and was immersed in some magazine. My client spoke before I got back to my seat.

'Does the name Mark Adams mean anything to you, Mr Faraday?'

I gave a low whistle. Mrs Van Gimpel nodded approval, folding and unfolding her fingers quickly.

'Just so, Mr Faraday. I see the name does mean something.'

'Millionaire for starters,' I said. 'Owner of racecourses and race-horses. Orchid fancier. Woman fancier too from what I hear. And other things.'

Mrs Van Gimpel went on nodding. Her voice was so low when she spoke I had a job to catch what she was saying.

'What other things, Mr Faraday?'

'Rackets,' I said. 'Nasty things. Dope, bordellos, numbers. That will do for starters. But the sort of man who knows how to keep his skirts clean. So we have to tread carefully.'

Mrs Van Gimpel drew in her breath with a little rasping noise like winter wind going through a hedgerow.

'So you can see how anxious I am about my daughter.'

'I can see,' I said. 'We have to approach this obliquely. Adams has a hatchet-man. He runs all the dirty ends. A man called Eli Tombes. If you can call him a man.'

Mrs Van Gimpel shivered suddenly, like there was a cold wind blowing through the room now.

'It's another world, Mr Faraday,' she said. 'I will pay anything to get my daughter out of this man's clutches.'

'What do you know?' I said.

Mrs Van Gimpel compressed her lips into a thin, straight line.

'Not a lot, Mr Faraday. I saw them together at the races one afternoon. They didn't see me. I studied them through my binoculars. I recognised him through newspaper photographs. Though the papers daren't say so openly they hint at unsavoury things.'

'Did you tackle your daughter about it?' I said.

The grey-haired woman was looking down through the big window. I followed her gaze, saw the girl was creaming across the pool, with long, lazy strokes.

'Valerie is no better than she should be,' she said dreamily. 'But she deserves something better than that. And I'm going to make sure she gets it.'

'You mean I'm going to make sure,' I said.

Mrs Van Gimpel's eyes flashed and she drew herself up. Then her expression softened.

'You are perfectly correct, Mr Faraday. And that means I must give you all the assistance I can. In the way of money, expertise and firepower. No, I haven't spoken to her. It wouldn't have done any good. I'll leave that to your discretion.'

I stared at her.

'Firepower? Meaning what?'

'Meaning Joseph, Mr Faraday. He has been with me a long time. I trust him as I would myself. He is an excellent amateur boxer. As well as a first-rate shot.'

I grinned.

'Before we talk logistics I need to know a lot more about the situation. More about Adams; about the girl's involvement. When and how they met; how far the thing has gone. I haven't said I'd take the case yet, come to that.'

Mrs Van Gimpel raised her eyebrows again. 'But you will take the case, Mr Faraday. After all, you've taken the money.'

I traded glances with her.

'You're being unfair, Mrs Van Gimpel. I can't afford not to take the case and you know it.'

I stared down at the garden, thinking of Mark Adams and Eli Tombes and all the stories running round L.A.

'Even if it means getting my butt shot off,' I said.

CHAPTER FOUR

1

'Mark Adams?' Stella said.

She looked incredulous.

'Wouldn't it be easier just to go out and get yourself run over by a beer-truck?'

'Easier, maybe,' I said. 'But not so profitable.'

I flipped over the envelope containing Mrs Van Gimpel's cheque. Stella studied it in silence. Her eyes looked very blue in the light of the late afternoon sun spilling through the blinds.

'Very nice, Mike. But you'll have trouble spending it if you're dead.'

'I'm leaving it to you, honey,' I said.

Stella bit her lip. She got off the desk with a rippling motion that set my nerves aflame.

'Coffee?'

'Try me,' I said.

She clittered over to the glassed-in alcove where we do the brewing-up.

I sat and watched her all the way, the plastic-bladed fan pecking at the brittle edges of the silence. Stella came back and sat on the side of my desk, swinging a bronzed knee. I studied the cracks in the ceiling, not concentrating very well.

'Ludwig of Bavaria, Mike. So that's where he got to. Up at Courtenay Estates?'

'Looks like it,' I said modestly. 'Though Mrs Van Gimpel's probably got more money than Ludwig ever saw in his lifetime.'

Stella still looked sceptical. She stared at me for a few moments longer and then went back to her coffee brewing. I sat on at my battered old broad-top, listening to the faint hum of the stalled traffic on the boulevard outside.

Stella was back again, staring down at me, the gold bell of her hair shining under the lamps.

'That negro butler sounds a nut, Mike.'

I shrugged.

'They're all nuts. And I'm the biggest nut for taking the case.'

Stella smiled. I could have watched it all evening. She picked up Mrs Van Gimpel's cheque. It made a stiff crackling sound.

'I'll put this in the bank first thing in the morning.'

'You do that,' I said.

I waited, closing my eyes, conscious of a patch of perspiration in the small of my back, until she came and put the coffee down on my blotter. She went around the desk and sat in the client's chair, cupping her chin in her hands. Today she wore a white dress of some crisp material with a plain brown belt and matching tan shoes.

It was all simple enough but the way it looked shot my morale to hell and back. She must have been aware of this because she smiled faintly as she reached over toward the biscuit tin. I rooted around for a couple of my favourite butter-nut fudge specials and stared down moodily toward the stalled traffic on the boulevard outside.

'So what's the case?' Stella said.

'We have this very rich lady,' I said. 'Head of San Rosario Corporation. And she has these two beautiful daughters.'

Stella crinkled up her nose as her gold pencil went racing across the paper.

'You should have taken your white charger out there, Mike.'

I ignored that, stirring my coffee, relishing the moment when I'd be savouring the first sip. Like I figured it was one of the best two moments of the day. The first was the morning brew, of course.

I went on for a couple of minutes, filling in the detail. Stella paused, pushing her pad on

28

one side and reaching out for her own cup. She drank in silence for a moment.

'So that's Tuxedo Park. It certainly seems to live up to its name.'

'You don't know the half,' I said. 'It's the sort of place where you have to present a chit to get off the estate for a haircut.'

Stella smiled. It seemed to light up the office.

'They have this negro butler straight out of *Gone With the Wind*,' I said. 'Except he can use a gun and is pretty handy in a roughhouse.'

Stella gurgled to herself. I'd described the fight to her earlier. If you could call it a fight.

'He was just holding back because of your age, I expect.'

'Thanks a lot,' I told her.

She smiled again and turned to her notebook.

'Those two girls,' I went on. 'The youngest is Valerie. She's about nineteen. The other's Erica. She's twenty-eight. I had that from her mother.'

The corners of Stella's mouth turned up slightly.

'It's important to be precise in such matters,' she told the filing cabinet.

I ignored that also. It was too hot an afternoon.

'The youngest girl got mixed up with Mark Adams,' I said. 'How deeply I haven't yet found out.'

Stella looked at me seriously.

'That means Eli Tombes.'

'The point hadn't escaped me,' I said.

'Anyway, I had this talk with the butler. He doesn't like either of the girls very much, though he's marginally in favour of Erica. He's fanatically devoted to Mrs Van Gimpel. He pledged me his support if it came to any heavy stuff.'

'That could be useful,' Stella said.

'Or a liability,' I told her. 'I put him out fairly easily.'

'He could have been soft pedalling,' Stella said.

I looked at her absently.

'That was his story. Where was I?'

'The faithful Tara retainer was pledging his support to the young master,' Stella said.

'You're turning this into a soap opera,' I said.

'You don't need any help from me,' Stella said.

I shut up then and concentrated on the coffee.

2

The light was deepening and the shadows dark on the window blinds when we finished kicking things around.

'What about these girls?' Stella said.

She got up and went over to the alcove to fetch me a second cup. I waited until she came back and put it down on my blotter.

'I didn't get to see them today,' I said. 'They'd both disappeared by the time I left Mrs Van Gimpel and I didn't want to spend the rest of the afternoon tramping over the estate.'

Stella looked down at the cheque at her elbow.

'So where do you start?'

I shrugged.

'Looks like San Rosario Corporation,' I said. 'They have an administrative building here in L.A.'

Stella nodded. She brushed an imaginary strand of gold hair back from her eyelids.

'I checked them out in the directory. All the information's here. You can look in on your way over tomorrow morning.'

She glanced at me quizzically.

'But won't that cause some comment?'

I shook my head.

'I wondered when you'd ask. Mrs Van Gimpel's given me carte blanche. I'm an executive vice-President, recently appointed, from the New York office, learning the ropes out on the West Coast.'

I flipped the impressive-looking envelope over.

'And I have documentary evidence to prove it.'

Stella studied the elaborately headed letter in silence. Then she put it back in the envelope with a faint crackling of expensive paper.

'So where does that get you?'

'Maybe nowhere,' I said. 'But who can tell? The lady's no fool. She built up the whole conglomerate.'

'She thinks Adams may be using the daughter to muscle into her business somehow,' Stella said. I looked at her for a long moment.

'She didn't say so,' I said. 'But you may have something.'

Stella shook her head in disbelief.

'That's what you pay me for.'

She put out her hand on the desk and closed her fingers over mine momentarily. They felt cool and reassuring against my skin. Then she withdrew them quickly.

'You'll go over there in the morning, Mike?' I nodded.

'I'll look in there, like you said. Leastways, it will save all the drag out to the estate for a day or two. Though I'll have to see the girls.'

'Who already know you're a private eye,' she pointed out.

'It hadn't escaped my notice,' I said. 'It was a dumb move on my part but when I met the girl at the pool it didn't occur to me that Mrs Van Gimpel's problems could have anything to do with them.'

'It can't be helped now,' Stella said.

She sat on at the desk in silence with that marvellous tact of hers. I lit a cigarette, savouring the coffee and thinking of Mrs Van Gimpel and her problems. Presently Stella got up, brought me a few letters to sign and hooded her typewriter. She paused at the door.

'I'll drop these in on my way home. Anything else you need?'

'Only my head examining,' I said.

She smiled faintly and I heard the clicking of her heels across the waiting room linoleum and the closing of the outer door. Then there was the distant whine of the elevator going down and I was alone with the hum of the traffic; the smog at the window panes; and the angry whine of a bluebottle. I picked up the *Examiner* and read it while I drank my coffee. There was nothing in it to set the town on fire. Not in my book anyway.

I finished the coffee and my cigarette and still sat on. I didn't know what the hell I was doing here watching the lengthening shadows at the window; listening to the distant hum of traffic; the sweat slowly trickling down the small of my back. Presently I looked at my watch. It was already half-six. I dragged myself over toward the alcove and rinsed my cup.

I went in the microscopic wash-room in back and ran my head under the tap. I felt better then. I remembered what Mrs Van Gimpel had said about the case being gun-stuff. I'd break out my favourite Smith-Wesson .38 from the small armoury I keep in a locked cupboard of my bedroom in my rented house over on Park West. I'd do that tonight before turning in.

I wouldn't have any need of it yet. But as soon as I started digging into the affairs of Mark Adams and Eli Tombes that made it a whole different ball game. But I'd speak to the Van Gimpel girls first. I went back to my desk and stood staring down vacantly at the blotter. Now that I came to think it over my client had given me more difficulties than leads.

Valerie Van Gimpel hadn't exactly impressed me at the swim-pool up at the house. She'd been distinctly sullen and arrogant. She already knew I was a gumshoe. And she wouldn't exactly welcome my probing her relationship with Adams. That left Erica. She'd looked even more cool and ritzy than her sister. I'd already blown my cover. And as soon as I spoke to one or other of the girls that would lead me straight to Adams and his friends. Who wouldn't be pleased. It looked like a canful of worms from where I was standing.

I gave it up for the night. I'd learned long ago it's no use going out to meet trouble. I'd sort it through tomorrow. I turned off the lights and left the office to its stale aroma of dusty dreams and the sordid little problems that had been aired there. I switched off the waiting room light and snubbed the main door catch.

I was still standing there when a shadow slipped between me and the corridor light. I was looking at a girl's face of extraordinary beauty, framed between two wings of soft gold hair.

'Forgive me, Mr Faraday, but I wanted to catch you alone.'

She held out a small brown hand for me to shake.

'We had a fleeting contact earlier in the day. I'm Erica Van Gimpel.'

CHAPTER FIVE

1

I stared at her for a long moment, the heat and tiredness suddenly seeming to recede.

'You'd better come on in,' I said. 'Or would you rather go somewhere for a drink?'

She smiled faintly. She was very tall and she wore white linen slacks with a rust-coloured shirt pulled in tightly across her finely formed breasts. She carried a polished leather bag suspended from a strap at her right shoulder.

'Why don't we make this an official talk first, Mr Faraday? Then, if you still want, we can have that drink after.'

I grinned.

'That sounds a very nice suggestion, Miss Van Gimpel.'

I led the way back through, buttoning the lights.

'I saw your secretary leave a while back. She's a lovely girl.'

I let that one go.

I waved her into the client's chair and went around to sit in back of my desk. She glanced swiftly round the office, her face inscrutable.

'Isn't much, is it?' I said.

She shrugged, putting her shoulder bag down on a corner of the desk.

'It depends on what you regard as important in life, Mr Faraday,' she said softly.

I studied her in silence for a moment.

'Just what is your idea of important things, Miss Van Gimpel?'

She crossed her long legs in the white linen slacks and traded glances levelly.

'Honesty, integrity, decent standards.'

'You think I might fit the bill?'

She tossed the hair back from her eyes in a gesture that reminded me of her sister.

'You've already passed muster, Mr Faraday. I know your track record.'

I looked over toward the window where red, yellow and green neon was beginning to stripe the blinds.

'With you or your mother?'

She smiled again.

'With both.'

'Is that why you're here?' I said. 'Because you admire my ethics?'

Her expression was frank and open now. 'Hardly, Mr Faraday. But it was one of the factors that impelled me to come this evening. So that we could have a talk.'

'Why?' I repeated.

She shrugged.

'Because I think it's important that we get a few things straight from the outset. I don't know what my mother's told you . . .'

I interrupted her before she could go on.

'Our business was private,' I said. 'I never reveal the client's affairs. We can only talk on that basis.'

Erica Van Gimpel raised her elegant eyebrows.

'I've already proved my point, Mr Faraday,' she said mockingly.

I didn't answer that, just waited for her to go on.

'I still think it's important we talk,' she went on after a bit. 'My mother's a very rich woman. A lot of people would like to get hold of her money. One easy way would be through my sister. She's very young and very impressionable.'

'I wouldn't disagree with that,' I said cautiously.

She thought for a moment, putting her head on one side, like she was listening for something in the silence of the empty building.

'I don't know what you discussed with my mother,' she said at last. 'And I wouldn't think of asking. But some strange things have been happening.'

I leaned back at my desk and reached for my pack of cigarettes. The girl declined my offer.

'I don't smoke. But go ahead, please.'

I did like she said, putting the spent matchstalk in the earthenware tray on my desk.

'Like what?' I said.

She put two slim hands round one white linen knee and rocked to and fro for a moment. For a fraction of time she reminded me of Stella. I tried to read what she was thinking but her features were as blank as my own thoughts on Mrs Van Gimpel's problems.

'It's my sister, Valerie, really,' the blonde girl said at last. 'I shouldn't really be saying this. But she's pretty wild and she may have gotten into bad company.'

I did my best to look surprised.

'I don't see how that concerns me.'

The girl twisted in the chair, like she was on the wrong tack.

'I only meant that while you're working for my mother, you might keep an eye on Valerie, too.'

'If it's within my purview, Miss Van Gimpel,' I said. 'You wouldn't care to enlarge on the bad company angle.'

The girl shook her head quickly.

'I think I've said enough, Mr Faraday. Perhaps too much.'

She bit her lip.

'It's only that I thought you might . . . That is, if it's not too much trouble . . . And doesn't interfere with your assignment.'

She let the words hang in the air, where they seemed to quiver in among my cigarette smoke.

'Fond of your sister, are you?' I said.

She made a little twisted mouth.

'Fond enough. But we've never been really close. There's nearly ten years between us, you see.'

She got up quickly, trying to hide her embarrassment.

'I'm sorry, Mr Faraday.'

I got up too and we stood looking at one another for a few seconds, while her brown eyes searched my face.

'It's all right,' I said. 'Let's go grab that drink.'

2

The sound of the jukebox, playing an old blues melody of the twenties seemed to hang in the air long after the vibrato saxophone notes should have dispersed. But that was maybe because of the smoky atmosphere in here and

39

the powerful effect the Van Gimpel number was having on me. The small bar was half-empty yet crowded with shadows thrown by the low wattage bulbs of the lantern ceiling fittings.

It was that sort of place but it was conveniently close to my office and reasonably empty this time of the early evening, which was why I had chosen it. The girl sat at the table across from me in the booth and toyed hesitantly with her drink. She'd drawn a lot of glances from lonely middle-aged men sitting up on bar-stools taking their fourth or fifth shots of sauce between their offices and the cocktail hour at their homes, but I guess she was used to that.

'Just why did you come to see me?' I persisted.

'Just curiosity, I guess. I was impressed with you out at mother's place.'

'You hardly noticed me,' I said.

She shook the long blonde hair back from her face impatiently.

'That's where you're wrong, Mr Faraday. I don't miss many things. Valerie told me you were a private detective so I looked you up in the book.'

She snagged her lip with very white teeth and put her glass down on the table in front of her.

'I thought mother was in some sort of trouble. Forgive me for prying. But it's a natural feeling.'

'Sure,' I said. 'And you were worried about your sister.'

The girl's eyes were fixed on my face now to the exclusion of everything and everyone else in the bar.

'That was indiscreet. I've probably said too much.'

I put down my glass.

'That's everyone's failing in this world. One either says too much or too little. It's never right.'

The girl smiled too.

'You're quite a philosopher, Mr Faraday.'

'So they tell me,' I said modestly.

'You were talking about strange things. I'd like to know more about that.'

The girl shook her head.

'But you told me your assignment was nothing to do with my sister. In which case there's no point.'

'It could have some relevance to my inquiries,' I said.

The girl stared at me for a long moment then seemed to make up her mind.

'Like I said, Mr Faraday, Valerie's a pretty wild sort of girl. But just lately things have become more extreme. She's always been an indiscreet drinker, from the age of sixteen. Now she's definitely out of control. And she stays out all night, sometimes.'

I took another nibble at my drink and sat

back against my padded banquette.

'It seems about par for the course these days,' I said. 'Kids get hooked on booze, sex and drugs from about eleven onwards.'

Erica Van Gimpel put her head on one side, her eyes fixed on the people sitting at the bar now. 'It's a horrible world, Mr Faraday,' she said softly.

'It's what you make it,' I said. 'Only there are a lot of people around who try to corrupt kids. For profit, of course. It's not a world I know much about, really. Though I brush against it from time to time in the course of my work.'

I put my glass back on the table.

'So what are you trying to tell me?'

The Van Gimpel number seemed to have come to a decision.

'All this may sound very trivial to you, Mr Faraday.'

'Nothing's trivial in my business,' I said.

The blonde number sipped moodily at her drink.

'You know how hard Courtenay Estates are to get into, Mr Faraday?'

'Not really, Miss Van Gimpel,' I said. 'I know there's a fence and a guard in a cubicle.'

The girl smiled.

'That's a very superficial assessment, Mr Faraday. You're not to know, of course. You've only been out there once. The man at the main entrance is merely one of about thirty guards and foot patrol people. The perimeter fence is guarded by sensors; there are infra-red cameras and closed circuit television. Dogs and armed guards patrol the miles of road and the individual estates; there's a central control room; mobile patrols in touch with each other's vehicles by walkie-talkie.'

'You could have fooled me, Miss Van Gimpel.' The girl tossed the hair back from her eyes. 'That's the idea, Mr Faraday. Courtenay Estates keeps a low profile. The security is very unobtrusive. That's the best kind of security. When you drove out today you were watched every yard of the way from the time you left the entrance gate.'

'I hope they got my best side,' I said. 'My left-hand profile is the one.'

The girl smiled faintly.

'You were a legitimate visitor, Mr Faraday. If you hadn't been, things would have been different.'

'I take it you're getting to the point,' I said. 'If there is a point.'

The girl's eyes flashed.

'There is a point, Mr Faraday,' she said softly. 'Like I told you my sister's mixed up in some very odd things. But I mustn't distract you if my mother's hired you for some other purpose.'

'I didn't say,' I told her. 'But I'm still interested.'

The girl put her two hands together on the

table in front of her; the bronzed pillars of her neck looked like the work of some master sculptor against the crispness of her shirt.

'I make the point for what it's worth. We're used to Valerie coming in at all hours, in various states of intoxication.'

'It's an old, familiar story,' I said.

'I was up late this night,' Erica Van Gimpel said. 'You can see clear to the edge of the property from the window of my bedroom. Valerie's car ran off the road near the main gate. I could hear her and a man arguing.'

I shrugged.

'All right, Miss Van Gimpel,' I said. 'What do you want me to say? Nothing out of the ordinary. A lover's quarrel.'

The girl slanted her eyebrows.

'Maybe, Mr Faraday. But then several shots were fired, right down where Valerie's car was.'

She got up suddenly, draining her glass.

'Valerie was obviously unhurt, because you've seen her since. I can't say any more. Firstly, because I don't know any more and I don't want to prejudice your operations.'

She stood over me, giving me a tight-lipped little smile.

'Please don't get up. I'm late for an appointment now.'

She walked a yard away as I rose from my seat automatically.

'But it's worth thinking about, wouldn't you

say?'

I nodded.

'I'll check it out if I get the chance.'

The girl smiled again.

'You do that, Mr Faraday. And thanks for the drink.'

She went on out, every male eye in the room on her. I sat and admired her action all the way to the main doors. I finished off my drink and ordered another from the platinum blonde waitress in the smart black and white dress.

It had long been dark when I quitted the bar and the lights of L.A. made a multi-coloured glare in the sky. I had a lot to think about as I drove home.

CHAPTER SIX

1

The San Rosario building, when I found it, turned out to be a jazzy chrome and marble building that reared thirty storeys to the sky of downtown L.A. I found a parking slot in the end and got out the Buick, the bulk of the Smith-Wesson making a faint pressure against my ribs in the nylon harness. It was hotter than ever today and I was sweating before I got halfway up the entrance steps, making for the shade of the awning.

I pushed open the big double doors and went across marble tiling into a concourse slightly larger than that of Grand Central Station. There were lots of blown-up colour photographs of Rosario's activities spread about in expensive cedarwood frames; the transparencies, lit from behind, showing every aspect of the Corporation's operations but I had no time for them this morning.

There seemed to be hundreds of extras about too, groomed in that obsessively perfectionist way that only people working in the high fashion industries affect. That goes for the males too. I felt distinctly poor-white before I'd gotten halfway to the reception desk where a dark-haired number with a Veronica Lake bang over one eye was buffing her nails and sneering at the cut of my suit.

From a metal-framed plaque on the counter in front of her I could see that her name was Monika During. She had three people queuing in front of her desk already so I took my place and studied her superstructure. She seemed to have been trained by the Mafia because she gave each client a frosty look; barked out some unintelligible command; and banged a bell-push at her elbow which brought women in dark dresses to conduct the clients away.

All the while making with the icy contempt and continuing with her nail-buffing operations. She was some operator. I didn't give her any chance to use the technique on me.

'I'm looking for Miss DuRose,' I said. 'My time's important so get her down here quick.'

While her mouth was still open in a round O of surprise I flourished Mrs Van Gimpel's letter. But her brain was still functioning because she was stabbing at the button like she had a nerve paralysed somewhere. One of the dark-dressed attendants materialised at my elbow.

The During woman unfroze her jaw.

'Take this gentleman to Miss DuRose,' she gurgled.

I leaned over the desk and gave her my best executive stare.

'You're dealing with people, Miss During,' I said. 'People. Just remember that.'

The little lady in the dark dress grinned suddenly. The During number visibly wilted and actually dropped the buffing board she'd been using on her nails. I walked away from the counter and then turned.

'I shall be getting reports of you, Miss During,' I said crisply. 'If I don't hear of any improvement there'll be some changes made.'

I thought the dark number's lower jaw was going to hit the counter but she didn't quite manage that. She gave me a frozen smile and the little blonde wheeled me forward toward the express elevators on the far side of the concourse. We got in another queue, my guide looking at me sidewise.

'I don't know your name, sir,' she began.

'It's Faraday,' I said. 'And don't call me sir.'

She smiled. She was remarkably pretty now I came to think of it.

'I'd just like to shake you by the hand, Mr Faraday.'

She must have noticed the surprise on my face but I put out my hand like she said. She pumped my arm up and down like she was never going to stop.

'What's all that in aid of?' I said when she let go my bruised fingers at last.

She passed a pink tongue across her full lips.

'It's that Monika During, Mr Faraday. It's been a long time . . .'

The sentence trailed off as her shoulders shook.

'Let me in on it,' I said. 'I'm new around here.'

The little girl had heightened colour now.

'It must be difficult for you to understand, Mr Faraday. But I've worked here for five years.'

I gave her a long look. The elevator doors were opening now and we were drifting forward.

'And?'

The little blonde leaned forward, her voice a whisper.

'I've been waiting all that time for her to get

her comeuppance.'

Her smile lasted her all the way to the eighth floor.

2

She was still making the most of it when she left me in a corridor that seemed to have been left over from the Hall of the Caliphs set from the old days of Universal-International when they were making with the Scheherazade stuff with Tony Curtis, Piper Laurie, Arnold Moss and such-like Eastern actors. There was a polished chrome door in front of me which said in gold lettering: CYNTHIA DUROSE: PERSONNEL DIRECTOR.

I pressed the buzzer set in the middle of the door and it slid sidewise, revealing another left-over set; this time from Things to Come. They were certainly mixing their styles around here. Their countries, come to that.

There was about an acre of polished black flooring before I got to Miss DuRose's white desk which was in the shape of a horseshoe. There were two other secretary's desks on the far side and a superb view of the smog and the L.A. landscape through the big circular windows in rear.

The willowy blonde who rose from behind the desk was slightly over six feet in height and beautifully built from what I could see. She came around the desk. She wore a lightweight suit of some shimmering material and her legs seemed to go on for ever. I had no time to dwell on them because her 2,000 candlepower smile was burning me up in mid-stride.

'Reception has just been on, Mr Faraday. You seem to have made quite a big impression.'

'That was the idea,' I said.

I'd decided to play along with Mrs Van Gimpel's idea and I was rather enjoying the contrast to my usual assignments. Cynthia DuRose was about twenty-eight with a complexion like the French soap ads and a delightful perfume that made one sag behind the knees. I don't know about women, of course. I was just registering her effect on me. But she looked at me guilelessly with steady grey eyes and led me to an uncomfortable-looking steel and leather chair set the other side of her desk.

'I thought it would be more discreet to have a private chat before you look around, Mr Faraday.'

'Sure,' I said. 'Just my idea.'

We were still standing the far side the desk and I got out Mrs Van Gimpel's letter; but the blonde number merely glanced at it absently, like she already knew its contents.

'That will hardly be necessary, Mr Faraday. Mrs Van Gimpel has already discussed the situation with me.'

50

She raised her right hand and examined her finger nails frowningly.

'She was most specific. You may be sure I shall give you a hundred and fifty per cent co-operation.'

I sat down gingerly in the chair. Contrary to expectation it was extremely comfortable.

'I'll enjoy that,' I said.

Miss DuRose smiled archly.

'I meant just that, Mr Faraday. Mrs Van Gimpel was insistent. If there is anything I can do to assist you have only to ask.'

'I should appreciate my own office,' I said.

'We have a suite for visiting executives,' she said. 'Complete with private secretary.'

She gestured subtly with one manicured hand.

'It is entirely at your disposal.'

She cleared her throat delicately.

'It adjoins my own office and has a connecting door.'

'That sounds even nicer,' I said.

The tall girl put her eyes discreetly on the floor and walked across to her desk. She had a beautiful action. She sat down elegantly on a corner of the desk facing me, showing a good deal of high powered leg. She was certainly giving me both barrels this morning.

'I don't make a habit of being inquisitive, Mr Faraday,' she began hesitantly. 'But I should appreciate a little direction from you.'

I was beginning to enjoy myself now.

51

'In what way?' I said.

The tall number again cleared her throat gently, in a well-bred way, like we were in some classy TV ad for high-grade coffee.

'As to the areas of our operation in which you are most interested.'

She moistened her lips with her tongue once more and looked at me expectantly.

'Finance,' I said firmly. 'That is my speciality.'

I was giving her a line, of course, but I'd kicked around some thoughts driving over this morning. I knew nothing about perfumes or high fashion and all that stuff; and a ten-year-old girl would have seen through me in minutes. But if they threw sheafs of figures at me I could always stall for time and take them away to examine at my leisure. And get a real accountant to go through them, if necessary. The more I'd thought about it the more I'd liked it.

I'd said the right thing apparently. Miss DuRose nodded and slid off the desk.

'That's fine, Mr Faraday. I guessed as much. Computers. You'll want our Dr Ross. Freddie Ross is in charge of computer operations.'

She put her blonde head on one side and gave me a look that I felt clear to my socks.

'But first we'll have coffee and get down to basics.'

CHAPTER SEVEN

1

'This way, Mr Faraday.'

Cynthia DuRose gave me another brilliant sunburst over her shoulder as she opened the door at the end of the long corridor. We went through into a lobby that seemed to be made entirely of metal. Everything was gun-metal grey; floor, walls, ceiling.

The only thing that broke the monotony was the white ceiling fittings for the lights; and the two desks for the armed security men who sat either side the big double doors that said: COMPUTER CONTROL ROOM. ABSOLUTELY PRIVATE.

The two hard-faced characters at the desks gave me frosty looks until the tall blonde had told them who I was. Then their expressions changed to dislike mingled with respect. One of them got up and put an oddly shaped key into the metal lock of the door. It slid back and I could hear him locking it after us as we went on into the blinding light beyond. Miss DuRose had to raise her voice slightly above the electronic chatter of the instruments.

'You must forgive us the melodrama, Mr Faraday. We have to take precautions.'

'Is all the Fort Knox stuff really necessary?'

I said. 'This is the tightest security I've yet
seen.'

The tall girl laughed.

'Absolutely, Mr Faraday. You'd be amazed
at what goes on in the computer world. The
precautions at Fort Knox are absolutely lax
compared to what we have here.'

I took a raincheck on it. She'd already given
me some handy information. If there was a tie-
up with Mark Adams here it couldn't have
come from the girl Valerie. It would have to be
someone on the inside. Prompted by the girl,
perhaps. It depended on what leeway was
given to the family of the owner.

I knew Valerie Van Gimpel had a sinecure
job at the Corporation's Headquarters here.
She was a secretary in the advertising
department. Mrs Van Gimpel wouldn't trust
her with anything higher at nineteen and she
was dead right. Doubly right after what Erica
had told me the previous night. But that still
hadn't disposed of my question. I would have
to go at it very tactfully. Better not to ask any
questions at all. Especially about Valerie
having access to the computer room; I'd just
use my eyes, like always, and hope something
would break.

But there'd be time; if I was going to have
my own suite around here like the blonde
number had said, there would be plenty of
time. She had me by the elbow now and was
steering me down between the aisles of shining

machines past metal benches where white-coated technicians worked at what looked like electric typewriter keyboards and frowned over long sheets of print-out material.

No-one even glanced up as we went by. It reminded me of the Machine Room in *Metropolis* from an old Fritz Lang movie retrospective on TV. Except that the machines were doing the work that the slaves performed in the film.

We stopped at a big desk the far side of the room, commanding a nice view of the smog and the blurred images of L.A. through the vast curved windows. They must have been of special glass and double-glazed because not a murmur came through from the outside. It was like watching a movie on which the sound-track had failed. The desk was empty and Miss DuRose bit her lip in annoyance.

'It looks like Dr Ross has stepped out, Mr Faraday. He didn't know we were coming, of course.'

'That's all right,' I said. 'My time's my own. But if you're busy . . .'

The girl shook her head. There was a faint smile on her face.

'Dead against the rules, Mr Faraday. No-one not on the permanent staff allowed unattended within the Computer Room.'

I raised my eyebrows.

'Not even me?'

The girl looked confused.

'Don't get me wrong, Mr Faraday. You have the highest authority. And you have only to ring Mrs Van Gimpel to override these instructions. It's just that we have so much secret information here. I'd rather introduce you formally to Freddie Ross. What arrangements you make between yourselves are entirely up to you.'

I nodded.

'I wouldn't dream of it, Miss DuRose. Ringing Mrs Van Gimpel, I mean. Let's play it by the book.'

I grinned.

'I wouldn't want to put the doctor out. I've met some of these computer geniuses on my rounds for the Corporation.'

The girl smiled again. She seemed relieved.

'That's very understanding, Mr Faraday. I'll have him paged if you'll just wait here a moment.'

She went over to one of the far benches and talked to a sleek, dark-haired girl who was checking through what looked like a stack of programmes ready to go on one of the machines. I moved over closer to Ross' desk. Everything was anonymous and impersonal as I knew it would be. But I remembered what Mrs Van Gimpel had said about gun-stuff; Mark Adams' reputation; and the girl Erica's story of shots in the night. The bulk of the Smith-Wesson made a reassuring pressure against my chest muscles as I turned back toward the blonde girl as she strode easily across the room toward me.

'It won't take a minute, Mr Faraday.'

The dark number gave me a curious glance as she got up, smoothing down her white coat with red-tipped finger-nails. She went over toward a glassed-in cubicle which had ADDRESS SYSTEM in gold letters on the door. She sat down at a desk inside and switched on a microphone. She mouthed noiselessly for a few seconds so I figured that was soundproof too.

The Control Room was probably not only the nerve-centre for the whole building and the San Rosario operations coast to coast but world-wide as well. That could be important to know. I'd find out in due course. We waited a few more seconds, the blonde girl cool and reassuring.

Then a tall, sandy-haired man with a worried expression appeared in a corridor that ran along behind the far bank of computers. Cynthia DuRose shot me a relieved glance.

'Things are looking up, Mr Faraday,' she said drily. 'Two minutes flat. Dr Ross is improving his timing.'

2

Freddie Ross, when I got to meet him, appeared just as agitated as his distant figure had hinted. He strode down the room, his white jacket crumpled and awry, his eyes alert and wary behind the thick pebble lenses of his glasses.

He had a thin smear of reddish mustache beneath his beaky nose which didn't improve him any and his handshake was damp and ineffectual.

'Forgive me, Mr Faraday,' he said, after the DuRose number had introduced us. 'It's a little hectic around here today.'

'You must forgive the intrusion,' I said. 'It's strictly business.'

'Eigh?'

He looked from me to the tall blonde with a subtle change of manner.

'Mr Faraday is Mrs Van Gimpel's special representative,' Cynthia DuRose said soothingly. 'A director from the East. He's to have absolute freedom to come and go.'

Ross' eyebrows shot up agitatedly and a little tic was beating at the side of his forehead. He looked helplessly from me to the girl.

'I don't quite understand . . .'

Before she could reply the sleek, dark-haired girl was at the doctor's elbow, waving a big buff envelope.

'There's the print-out material you wanted for this evening, Dr Ross.'

For some reason the sandy-haired man turned white around the eyes and looked distinctly embarrassed. He mumbled something, took the envelope and thrust it hurriedly into a drawer of his desk. This was getting more entertaining by the second; but I just kept staring at the doctor, conscious that there was something wrong here that I couldn't yet read but which might make sense if I worked at it.

'You were saying, Dr Ross?' the DuRose number went on smoothly.

'Mr Faraday. You say he is Mrs Van Gimpel's personal representative?'

I got out the letter the client had given me and held it in front of his eyes. He seemed visibly to crumple as he read it. He had to clear his throat three times before he could make with a normal sentence.

'Glad to be of help, Mr Faraday. But I don't quite see your function here.'

I gave him one of my best smiles. The thin-lipped type like Humphrey Bogart. The ones I'd been practising in front of the mirror.

'Security. Financial control. Possible improvements. You know the sort of thing.'

Ross didn't exactly drop anything but the pipe he'd taken from the pocket of his white coat trembled in his slim fingers.

'You were hinting it was a little hectic,' I went on before he could recover himself. 'What's going on?'

Ross had hold of himself now.

'A new installation, Mr Faraday. The 4FT. You are familiar with it?'

I had perhaps two seconds. Both Ross and

59

the DuRose number had their eyes glued on my face.

'No,' I said, hoping it was the right answer. I'd come up with the proper response apparently. Ross' face cleared.

'I'm not surprised, Mr Faraday. It's the first of a new generation. Only just out. We're trying to wire it up next door. That's why I was away from my desk.'

He mopped his forehead with a red silk handkerchief, leaving a thin glaze of sweat below the sandy hair.

'You worry too much,' I said.

I had my gaze fixed on his top desk drawer and I fancy I saw his eyes twitch behind the big pebble glasses. It was difficult to make out because of the overhead lights glinting on them. He licked his lips with a bluish tongue. His voice sounded so dry it was like crackling paper.

'Something wrong, Mr Faraday?'

I shook my head.

'I hope not. Just routine. I'm making the rounds of all the San Rosario establishments.'

I was beginning to sound convincing, even to myself. Ross and the DuRose number evidently had no doubts about my bona fides. Why should they, when I had a letter signed by Mrs Van Gimpel in my pocket. Ross shifted awkwardly from one foot to another.

'I don't quite see what I can do, Mr Faraday. Our work is so technical.'

'I'd just like facts and figures,' I said. 'Plus something signed by you so that I can come and go as I please without all the Bastille stuff.'

Ross exchanged a look with the blonde girl and licked his lips again.

'Shouldn't be too much trouble about that, Mr Faraday. So long as you don't actually touch any of the equipment.'

I laughed then.

'There's no danger of that, Dr Ross. It's all far too complicated for a layman like me.'

The relief was evident on Ross' face.

'That's all right then, Mr Faraday. I'll write you something straight away.'

He put himself into top gear, seating himself at the desk and writing on a sheet of headed notepaper with concentrated ferocity. Miss DuRose excused herself with a smile.

'I see you're all fixed up, Mr Faraday. If there's anything you want you know where to find me. I'll take you along to your office when you're ready.'

'Fine,' I said.

She went on out with a clittering of heels. Not one of the white-coated technicians turned his head. They were a strange breed in here. I decided computer technology wasn't my scene. Not if it led to such atrophy of the senses. I watched the girl out the door.

Ross' pen went on scratching over the paper. He picked up a stamp and hammered it on the document with a self-important flourish. Then he added his signature over the top like it would increase the value of the thing.

'I think that will do the trick, Mr Faraday.'

I took it from him, read it through and then folded it before putting it in my pocket. Ross got up and gave me his hand to shake like we'd just signed the Treaty of Rome.

'I'll leave you to it now,' I said. 'I have to find my way around the building. But I'll be back.'

Ross looked uncomfortable again.

'Sure, Mr Faraday.'

'Give my regards to the 4FT,' I said.

I went on out and left him there, a rumpled-looking figure among the chatter of the instruments.

CHAPTER EIGHT

1

I sat back at my desk and doodled on my scratchpad, taking my time about it. The office Cynthia DuRose had assigned me was such a contrast to my normal style of life I'd decided I might take it up permanently. It was more eighteenth-century with its rosewood panelling, elegant furniture, thick carpet and bowls of flowers. It helped my thinking considerably. Not that I had any thoughts on Mrs Van Gimpel's assignment that made much sense. Or any sense come to that.

But I'd spent an interesting if innocuous day. I'd toured the various sections of the San Rosario Corporation H.Q. and met the departmental heads. They'd all seemed pretty nervous after learning my ostensible mission, which couldn't have been a bad thing.

I'd had an excellent lunch in the commissary with the DuRose number and her own private secretary, which was even better. After lunch I'd gone back to the Computer Room on my own, giving Dr Ross another case of the jitters; had a hand-crafted tour of the installations; and even met the 4FT in person, which hadn't left me much the wiser. The brute took up most of a suite specially built next the Control Room and apparently needed about fifteen technicians to keep it fed.

It didn't seem very exciting to me but it had sent up Ross' blood pressure another four points, because they were still having teething problems. After that I'd gone back to my office and killed a little time by phoning Stella. I hadn't said anything important in case anyone might be listening in. I had nothing important to tell her but there was no need to tip my hand down here.

After that it was tea-time, taken with Miss DuRose and the same private secretary in her office. It was now a quarter of five and I was scribbling a few points down for my own edification. Besides, I had to look busy in case anyone else looked in. The points didn't add up to much. But then I hadn't expected them to.

I sighed and stared at my notations again. They read:

1   Mrs Van Gimpel's daughter Valerie has gotten into bad company, tying up with a known racketeer, Mark Adams. Possible business infiltration here.

2   Elder daughter, Erica, speaks of Valerie's incoherent life-style; shots fired when girl's car went off road. Check with gateman at Courtenay Estates.

3   Valerie works at San Rosario Corporation in minor capacity. Four floors down. Necessary, therefore, not to advertise my presence here.

4   Valerie knows I am a P.I. as does Erica. Obvious, therefore, that both Adams and his hatchet-man Eli Tombes know also; or will do shortly.

5   Dr Ross, chief computer and financial wizard at San Rosario nervous and ill at ease. Key man. Watch him.

Unless I was even more comatose than I felt this afternoon, that was about it. I screwed up the paper into a ball and put it in my pocket. I got up and stared round the office. It wanted but a few minutes of five.

I stabbed the button connecting me with Miss DuRose and told her I was going back to my hotel. I'd arranged a front with Stella and the hotel would have messages relayed to her. After that I said goodnight, put the phone down, left the office and rode the elevator down to the ground floor, seeing no-one I knew.

It was raining slightly when I got outside and the sky was overcast but the coolness was welcome after the heat of the day. I went down the parking lot quickly. I should have checked before but the idea had only just hit me. It took me only a few minutes because, like I figured, Ross' heap was parked up in the fairly small upper echelon executive section of the lot. He was driving a rather flashy-looking scarlet sedan with L.A. licence plates.

I checked on the details strapped around the steering post and went back to the Buick, winding down the windows to let out the heat of the day. I was getting nice and damp by this time. When the atmosphere inside was a little more bearable I got behind the wheel, wound up the window a fraction and set fire to a cigarette.

I listened to the monotonous drumming of the rain on the roof and watched the flawed neons start winking through the blur of moisture on the windshield. I sighed. This looked like being a long and non-productive one. I eased back in my seat and settled down to wait.

2

It was just after half-five before Ross showed. He was wearing a white raincoat now which looked remarkably like the long coat he'd worn in the Computer Room atop the San Rosario Building. He had a briefcase in his left hand and a large brown envelope in his right that resembled the one the girl had given him that morning. I decided it might be worth it after all.

I sank back in my seat and watched him out the side window as he went hesitantly down the aisle of parked cars to the scarlet sedan. He didn't glance right or left and seemed more absorbed with his inner thoughts than with the noise and hassle of L.A. around him. I waited until I saw blue exhaust smoke coming from his heap and then fired my own motor. I let him get to the edge of the lot before I eased out after him.

We drove for about half an hour across town and the rain was much heavier before we reached his destination. I'd kept several automobiles behind just in case he was on the look-out but I was convinced he didn't know he was being tailed. He wasn't that type of character. In the end he pulled up in front of a small bar whose shimmering blue neon spelled

66

out RIBERO'S through the stream of water on my windshield.

I drove on around the block, making sure in my rear-mirror that he was making for the bar. When I'd seen him inside I turned left at the next intersection and circled back, finding a slot about a hundred yards off Ross' heap before killing the Buick's motor. I sat and smoked another cigarette, giving him time to settle down. Maybe he'd just called in for a quick snifter on his way home. Then again, maybe not. He'd still had the brown envelope with him and that could mean something.

The rain was coming down steadily by the time I finished the cigarette and sprinted across to Ribero's. There was piped muzak playing some faintly nostalgic blues number of the thirties and a lot of dimly-lit booths inside. The only real light was up near a horseshoe-shaped bar at the far end. There was a waitress service which suited me fine because I might just as well have had myself paged if I'd had to walk all the way up there.

I got in a booth near the entrance which would suit my purposes. I'd already spotted Ross. He had his back to me and obviously hadn't seen me because there was no mirror on the facing wall. He was doing his best to make himself inconspicuous and he hadn't even bothered to take his raincoat off. He sat hunched forward dejectedly, his glass untasted at his side, his chin supported by his left hand.

There was no-one at the table with him.

The waitress came up and I ordered a beer and a double-decker sandwich. She was a bleached blonde in her early forties but she had a sensational figure beneath the tight gingham dress and she knew it. My eye was drawn to her swaying gait all the way down the big room. She went first to the bar to order the beer and then on to the swing-doors of the kitchen.

I kept my eye on Ross in an unobtrusive way but he sat on immobile, taking occasional sips at his glass. The jazzy blonde was back now, her full mouth wide in a professional smile, revealing excellent teeth. She seemed inclined to linger but I had other fish to fry and when I'd thanked her, I started to get outside the sandwich straight away. It might be the only thing I'd get to eat tonight. The irregular hours are one of the worst things about my racket.

I'd worked through the sandwich and ordered another beer before anyone showed. I wasn't aware of it at first, because he seemed to drift over to Ross' table almost as insubstantial as mist. I looked up to see a tall, silver-haired man in a check suit sitting down opposite the doctor in the shadowy booth.

His hair was cut in an unsuitably young style which accentuated his overhanging brow and the rat-trap smile flashed to reveal capped dentures, making the second tribute to insincerity I'd seen in the last half hour.

I shaded my face by leaning on my hand but they had no time for me. Rat-trap was already opening the big brown envelope Ross had given him. The computer expert seemed excited about something but the silver-haired man brushed his expostulations aside.

He was going through the long sheets of paper with concentration, his forefinger tracing out the characters. I recognised the material as the type of computer print-outs I'd seen at the San Rosario Corporation Building that morning. Or at least something very like them. Either way it was extremely interesting. I'd seen enough. There was no point in pressing my luck.

I finished up my second beer and unobtrusively beckoned the waitress over, making sure she shielded my face from the occupants of the booth opposite while we talked. I gave her a generous tip from Mrs Van Gimpel and her smile opened up another three millimetres. If one included Miss DuRose, I was getting a lot of high-class dental work today.

The two men in the booth were still absorbed in the computer print-out, their heads bowed over the figures, their foreheads almost touching. I melted out of Ribero's sidewise, my head turned away and got back in the street. It was dark now, the neons making a blurred Murillo of the wet sidewalks. I got over toward the Buick fast, unconscious of the slashing rain. I unlocked the driving door and slumped behind the wheel, reaching for my package of cigarettes.

I was still sitting there, my mind trying to concentrate above the soft drumming of rain on the roof, when the windshield starred into a thousand mosaics and something struck the interior cushions so violently that the Buick rocked back on its springs. I went down sideways as the second shot disintegrated the screen farther along.

CHAPTER NINE

1

Fear coursed through me like quicksilver as I reached for the Smith-Wesson. I couldn't make it because I was pressed down into the squab on my left side. A third shot smacked into the bodywork with a vicious spanging noise and I could smell burning now. I lifted myself, pulling the gun clear. I realised then it was nothing more serious than my match which was scorching the rubber mat on the floor of the automobile.

For a moment I thought one of the slugs had reached the tank. I flipped the headlamp switch with my left hand, the yellow beams scything through the darkened parking lot. They briefly caught the figure in the white slicker crouched at the edge of the dark sedan. I got off a shot with the Smith-Wesson through the half-open driving door. It went high but it scared the hell out of the marksman.

He dived behind the wheel and started the motor as I got out the Buick, keeping low. He went away fast down the lot, without lights, taking pounds of rubber off the tyres. I got off one more shot as I saw the sedan profiled against lighted windows the far side of the boulevard. But I was nervous and off balance and that went high too, way up in the branches of the trees fringing the lot.

The car was a dark blur against the lights and the driving rain and I saw the headlamps flick on as he got a couple of blocks away, too far for me to make out the licence plate. I got back in the Buick and reached for my pack of cigarettes, remembering to switch off my mainbeam. The match was still burning and I must have put it out with the edge of the pack because I found the match-stalk still there when I got back to Park West. My fingers were trembling very slightly as I lit up, my face pale and sardonic in the rear-mirror. I re-loaded the Smith-Wesson from the spare clip in the holster and put it down on the passenger seat at my side.

My nerves were so shot I almost went up through the roof when there came a tapping on the side window. I lowered the Smith-Wesson and put it quickly back in my shoulder holster. There was a white face staring in. I got out quickly, into the darkness and the driving rain.

'My God, mister. You were lucky.'

The character in the dark slicker was trembling so violently he could hardly stand.

'You're dead right there,' I told him.

I opened the passenger door and sat him down, he was so agitated.

'Thanks,' he mumbled. 'I've never seen anyone come so close to it before.'

He was a small, narrow-shouldered bald-headed man with his pate and his gold pince-nez shimmering with drops of rain in the light of the instrument panel. He looked from the shattered windshield and then to me with concern.

'You know who it was, sir?'

I shook my head, taking a deep pull at my cigarette.

'L.A.'s a violent place. Characters take pot-shots at people just for the fun of it.'

The little man shuddered.

'You're sure right there. I thought maybe I could help.'

I nodded.

'It was kind of you. But there was no need for two of us to get shot.'

The bald-headed man shivered again.

'You want me to call the police?'

I shook my head.

'I'll look in at my nearest station on the way home. Not that it will do any good.'

The little man grunted, reaching for his pince-nez with trembling hands.

'Can I drop you off anywhere?' I said.

He shook his head.

'It's kind of you, sir, but I have my car over there.'

He uncorked himself from the passanger seat stiffly and held out his hand. His face was less pale now.

'Take care how you drive. I should have that fixed as soon as you can.'

'I'll look after it,' I promised him.

I sat and finished my smoke, waiting until he'd got back to his automobile and driven off out. It was good of him to come over and I should maybe have thanked him a little more warmly if I hadn't been off balance myself.

I got my handkerchief, wrapped it around my fingers and cautiously enlarged the hole in the windshield. I was so cold and wet by the time I reached Park West it was an excuse for a stiff shot of bourbon.

2

Stella looked at me anxiously.

'You were lucky, Mike.'

'I believe you said that before,' I told her.

73

She smiled faintly.

'And I'm repeating it now.'

It was cooler this morning after the rain and the sun was making stippled shadows at the blinds. The motion of the plastic-bladed fan went on eroding the edges of the silence. The bulk of the Smith-Wesson made a comforting pressure against my chest muscles as I leaned back at my old broadtop and stared at the cracks in the ceiling.

'What about the Buick?' Stella said.

'It's being checked out,' I said. 'Shouldn't take more than an hour to fit a new windshield.'

Stella looked at me dubiously.

'They're supposed to report things like bullet holes,' she said.

I grinned.

'This is a discreet outfit. They won't report it. Besides, the slugs only made three small holes in the cushions.'

Stella shivered slightly and got up from her desk. She went over to the glassed-in alcove and started fussing with cups and saucers. She put her head round the screen.

'You don't know who shot at you or why, of course?'

'What makes you think that?' I said innocently.

Stella made an elegant little noise which passes for a snort with her.

'Shouldn't you be at the San Rosario

Building?' she said.

'I asked Miss DuRose for the morning off,' I told her.

Stella smiled. I couldn't see her but I knew all right.

'Those shots up at Mrs Van Gimpel's place . . .' Stella said.

She'd strolled back and was looking down at me with her arms folded.

'How come the guards didn't hear them?' she went on.

I shook my head.

'I haven't overlooked it, honey. It needs checking.'

Stella gave me another of her faint smiles.

'It isn't the only thing that needs checking on this case.'

I shifted in my chair.

'You do admit we have a case, then?'

Stella nodded slowly.

'Trouble is, there's too many possibilities.'

I didn't answer that. She had a point though. I sat on, tossing a few odds and ends around in my mind, waiting for her to show with the coffee. She put the cup down on my blotter and pushed over the biscuit tin. I rooted around for some of my specials while she went to fetch her own cup. She looked at me with very blue eyes.

'So Dr Ross is passing over San Rosario financial secrets to Mark Adams?'

I shrugged.

'Certainly looks like it. He's a pretty agitated character.'

Stella tapped very white teeth with her gold pencil.

'So might you be if you had to deal with Eli Tombes, Mike. He's the gritty end of Adams' operation.'

'So they tell me,' I said.

Stella sipped thoughtfully at her coffee.

'So what do you make of it all, Mike?'

'I was going to ask you,' I said.

She stared at me in that disconcerting way of hers.

'You can do better than that. You were watching Ross and Eli Tombes in the bar. Someone else was watching you. What does that suggest?'

'A hell of a lot of loose ends,' I said.

Stella took a note or two on her scratchpad and put her pencil down. She added a mite more sugar to her coffee.

'You sure that man didn't take your car number?'

I stirred my coffee with a thin, brittle noise that made a marked contrast to the distant rumble of traffic from the boulevard outside.

'I'm not sure about anything,' I said. 'If he did I'd have heard from the boys in blue before now. They have computers too.'

Stella smiled faintly. Today she was wearing a lightweight grey two-piece over a blue silk open-neck shirt. Like everything Stella just

76

happened to throw on it looked right.

'So you've no ideas?' she said in the end. I shook my head.

'Nothing that makes much sense.'

She was silent for a few minutes so I worked my way through the coffee. She got up in the end to fetch me a second cup. She put it down on the blotter, skipped out before my roving hand made contact.

Like always, in fact. She went round the desk and gave me one of her straight-faced looks.

'So what will you be doing today? Just in case anyone rings in?'

'They won't,' I said.

I looked over to the smog at the window and the stalled traffic on the boulevard beyond.

'But just for the record there are two possibilities. Either I'll be putting in another hard afternoon at the offices of the San Rosario Corporation. Or I'll be going up to Tuxedo Park.'

I grinned at Stella reflectively.

'I'm going to toss for it.'

CHAPTER TEN

1

In the end I went up to Mrs Van Gimpel's. There were a few things I wanted to check on. And it was true I wasn't yet ready to tangle with Mark Adams. Not before I'd had another talk with Valerie. I had a lot of no-facts knocking around inside my skull and it would be like throwing myself over a cliff in the dark. So I needed to scout out the ground first.

The garage had made a good job of the windshield and there couldn't have been more than a pound or two of glass crystals crunching around beneath my feet. I'd get them to vacuum it out the next time I took it in. Which would be no later than this evening.

There were still three holes in the rear upholstery but they couldn't be helped. I guessed I'd get them fixed some time. In the interim they were a visual reminder to be cautious.

I really should have someone take the slugs out. Not that I had any weapon to match them up with. But it might come in useful some time. I'd take a rain-check on it. The weather was still holding and I had a pleasant, sunny drive up to the estate. I kept my eyes peeled in the rear mirror all the way but there didn't seem to be anyone tailing me.

Not that there should have. But I'd been given one warning. If you could call it a warning. The person who'd fired those shots in the parking-lot had intended to take my head off. He'd damned near succeeded too. So I was handling things with kid gloves from now on.

I made good time to Tuxedo Park and it was only a little after three when I hit the main entrance. The same guard was in the sentry box but by the grim set of his mouth I might have been a complete stranger. He nodded frostily as I got up close but he hadn't forgotten.

'Mr Faraday for Mrs Van Gimpel, right? You expected?'

I shook my head.

'I'd like to ask you something before I go up.'

The guard looked at me warily with level grey eyes.

'Go ahead. But I don't guarantee to answer.'

'That's understood,' I said. 'I wouldn't expect you to do it for nothing.'

He stared at me without speaking.

'I'd like a straight answer,' I said.

The man in the booth nodded.

'Go ahead.'

'I understand there were some shots fired up on the estate a short while ago,' I said. 'Late at night.'

The eyes had subtly changed now. They were cold and watchful.

'What are you, mister? Private dick?'

I nodded. There was no point in denying it. He had me pegged. The sun was hot and heavy on my head as I moved over to the glass booth and showed him the photostat of my licence. He licked his lips nervously, looking back up the great sweep of road that shimmered in the heat.

'There could be trouble over this,' he said quickly.

I shook my head.

'No trouble. I'm working for Mrs Van Gimpel. She's a little worried, that's all. It won't get back to the people who run the estate, if that's what you're implying.'

I put the fifty bucks of Mrs Van Gimpel's money down in a little pile of low denomination notes on the shelf of his cubbyhole. He couldn't keep his eyes off it.

'There's no need for that, mister.'

I shook my head.

'The labourer is worthy of his hire.'

He looked around again.

'And you're sure this will be discreet?'

'A clam is gabby compared to me,' I assured him.

He gave a watery smile and the notes seemed to melt across the shelf into his uniform pocket.

'I was on duty that night,' he said, speaking

out the side of his mouth. 'I heard the shots. They were a long way off but it was a fine, still night and I had the door of the booth open because I was outside taking a smoke. I went through all the correct procedures, put the guards on alert. A thorough search was made.'

'They found nothing?' I said.

The guard shook his head.

'Nary a sign of an intruder. A guy came out about half an hour later. We got a machine here for detecting firearms without people knowing. I ran it over him. He was clean.'

'He came in with Miss Van Gimpel?' I said.

The man in the box scratched his head reflectively.

'I don't know everyone up here, Mr Faraday. And I'd rather not say, if you understand me. But this guy drove a very striking blonde girl home in this classy English sport-job. They went to the Van Gimpel estate. Put it like that.'

'I got you,' I said. 'What was this character like?'

Again the slow, reflective look from the gateman.

'Good-looking. Hard. About forty-five. Tall, blond character. That fill your bill?'

I nodded.

'Fine,' I told him. 'Anything else you can remember?'

He grinned briefly.

'I think you got your money's worth, Mr

Faraday. But, if it helps your petty cash figures, I've told you all there is to know.'

'You've been a big help,' I said.

'And not a word of this gets back? It could cost me my job otherwise.'

I shook my head.

'Scout's honour. Your pension's safe enough.'

His eyes were reflective as he picked up the phone.

'I got to report you, Mr Faraday, and let Mrs Van Gimpel know you're on your way. But I'll break a rule and let you through now.'

'I appreciate it,' I told him. 'Before you know it we'll be on first name terms.'

His thin smile in my rear-mirror lasted me almost the length of the first stretch of roadway.

2

I stopped the Buick at the entrance of Ashley Wilkes' place and went over the ground carefully. If what Erica Van Gimpel had told me was true there should be some visible traces of her story, despite the recent rain. It took me a few minutes of casting up and down but I found something in the end. The girl hadn't exaggerated.

I got down below the level of the ornamental bushes, aware that I must look pretty peculiar if there had been anyone watching. In the far distance the noise of the big mower went on. A place the size of Mrs Van Gimpel's must need almost round-the-clock maintenance. There was a tyretrack here, about ten yards inside the main gate.

The tread veered off to the left, making distinct V-impressions in the turned earth; the rain had only exaggerated the pattern, if anything. The driver of the vehicle had stopped after a yard or so and the edge of the driveway had been abraded by the weight of the automobile as the machine was reversed. A couple of bushes had been flattened too and they were just in process of getting back to the vertical.

It took weeks sometimes when plants had been badly crushed. I straightened up, conscious of perspiration beginning to trickle down the small of my back. The sun beat down like a hammer through the dappled shade of the trees and even the birds were fairly silent. I went back to stand in the middle of the driveway, my shadow long and heavy at my feet.

I glanced at my watch. I oughtn't to be too long because Mrs Van Gimpel would be expecting me and the gateman had already phoned her at least five minutes ago. But I had a hunch about the situation and I wanted to try it out. I worked a little back from the edge of the driveway, trying to envisage the exact position of the stalled automobile.

There was just a possibility that I might find something. It was a thin one but it was all I had for the moment. And if my feeling was right it could lead to something useful. There was a big stand of trees at the right-hand side of the drive going up just opposite where I was stationed. It was obvious that the builders of the estate had wanted to preserve them because the drive curved gently around to leave the nearest trunks some eight or ten feet back from the edge.

There was another turned bed between the tarmac and the trunks of the trees and I went across and gave it the onceover. No-one had trodden there and there were no marks of feet the other side where the car had gone over, so far as I could see. I stared at the trees for a moment longer. There was a magnificent oak in the centre of the group which must have been at least ten feet across.

I went back the other side of the driveway and worked out the angle made by the tyre-gouge in the soft earth. It lined up fairly well with the trees; particularly the oak which looked as broad as a house and too hard to miss. It was worth a try at least.

I went over the rough bark, taking a swathe between five and ten feet from the ground. It didn't take long and I hit the jackpot almost the first time off. There were two punctures which might be what I was looking for, around six inches apart, in the bark about seven feet from the ground. Something glinted in the nearest hole as the sunlight caught it.

I went back to the Buick and rummaged around in the boot. Nothing moved in all the wide brightness of the afternoon except for a distant speck in the sky which might have been a light aircraft circling somewhere out to sea. I went back with the steel screw-driver and eased out what was lodged in the bark. Oak's a hard wood but this one seemed to be jacketed in steel and the slug had penetrated only about half an inch below the bark.

I didn't bother about the other. The one I'd got wasn't too flattened and would do nicely. I put it in an old envelope I found in my wallet and replaced it in my breast pocket. I went and put the screw-driver back with the tool-kit in the boot and closed it up. I was still standing there, thinking about Erica Van Gimpel and the strange household out here when I became aware that someone was watching me.

It's a sixth sense most people have but it's very highly developed in P.I.'s; it has to be because sometimes it means the difference between life and death. It wasn't that sort of feeling this afternoon but I gave my well-known impersonation of a casual tourist and worked my eyeballs over the side of the drive, section by section.

Then I caught the white flash of a face and a strand or two of tawny hair. Their owner went away quietly, on the balls of her feet, going faster as she got farther off. I didn't bother to follow; I'd seen enough to know it was Valerie Van Gimpel who'd been standing there.

I could feel her wild eyes in the small of my back all the way up the curving drive to Xanadu.

CHAPTER ELEVEN

1

Mrs Van Gimpel was on the terrace when I got there; heavily gloved, armed with secateurs and pruning roses like fury from a low padded chair.

Despite her disability she got up and walked down the steps to meet me, leaning heavily on her stick.

'You shouldn't have bothered,' I said.

She shook her head. She wore a wide-brimmed straw hat to shade her face from the sun and it was difficult to make out her expression.

'You don't understand, Mr Faraday. If I sit for a long time in one position I get locked. Then it's worse. The exercise is good for me.'

I went back down the steps with her to where the Buick was parked. One of the gardeners was in sight now, seated on the scarlet mowing machine.

'You have some news for me, Mr Faraday,' she said.

Her voice was firm enough but there was just the faintest tremor at the end of the sentence.

'How did you know?' I said.

She shrugged, an ironical smile on her lips.

'Let's just call it women's intuition. Besides, if it had been routine you would have rung for an appointment. Not just come all the way out here.' She looked at me sharply, shading her eyes with the back of her hand from the sun.

'How did you know I'd be here?'

'I didn't,' I said. 'I took a chance. Besides, there were a few things I wanted to check on and I couldn't do that unless I went over the ground.'

She nodded, her eyes seeming like they were focused on the far distance.

'We'd best go on up to the house for tea,' she said. 'We can talk privately there. Or would you like to have something by the pool?'

'The pool would be fine,' I said.

I had a sudden flash of Valerie Van Gimpel, topless, her body arcing effortlessly through the water. Then I remembered she should have been at the San Rosario Corporation this afternoon. Instead of skulking at the end of the drive. Something else struck me then. Why hadn't she been at her office yesterday?

Unless she was currently on holiday. I filed

the query along with all the other rubble that passes for thoughts in the attic of my brain and adjusted my pace to Mrs Van Gimpel's laboured gait. Her face was screwed up with the concentration and I had a quick stab of pity for her situation. All the money in the world didn't compensate for such a crippling ailment.

We were passing the Buick and I walked over quickly and opened the near-side door. I indicated the rips in the rear seat upholstery. Mrs Van Gimpel bent over, her eyes concentrating with difficulty, adjusting to the dimness of the interior after the glare of the sun.

'What did that?' she said eventually.

'Moths,' I told her.

She chuckled, with a return to her old manner. Then she glanced at the fragments of glass beading on the floor around the driving seat. She braced herself with her stick like she was expecting a physical blow. I shut the door again.

'Let me have it, Mr Faraday,' she said gently. 'I wouldn't blame you if you didn't want the case.'

'You don't know what happened yet,' I said.

She shook her head.

'I gave you 3,000 dollars as a retainer, Mr Faraday. I also told you gun-stuff was involved. That meant the case was dangerous.'

I nodded.

'You were right. Someone tried to take me out last night. He put three shots through the windshield. At least two of the slugs lodged in the back squab. I don't know what happened to the other. If my reflexes hadn't been good I'd have been on a slab in the morgue right now.'

Mrs Van Gimpel shivered. She produced a small chrome box from a pocket in the gardening overall she was wearing. She spoke into it.

'You can come and collect me now, Joseph. We will have tea by the pool.'

There was a faint whirring noise almost before she put the walkie-talkie back into her pocket. A large electric golf trolley with balloon tyres came crunching over the gravel, the negro butler Joseph immaculate in a white duck suit, grave-faced behind the wheel. I helped Mrs Van Gimpel into the passenger seat.

'I am sorry there is room for only one, Mr Faraday. I will see you at the pool.'

I smiled.

'Sure. I think I can make it.'

The golf buggy purred into the hazy distance as I started back up the steps.

2

Mrs Van Gimpel bent down from her lounging

89

chair and dabbled her hands in the water of the pool. Like I figured we were alone up here. I sat beneath the shade of one of the ornamental umbrellas and watched her.

'Gardening gloves keep out the dirt all right, Mr Faraday, but one tends to perspire this weather.'

'Carry on,' I said.

Mrs Van Gimpel finished rinsing her hands and sat upright, small droplets of water dripping from her fingers and making golden flashes in the sunlight. I got up and put the low table between her chaise-longue and my cane-backed chair. The grey-haired woman looked at me with very penetrating eyes.

'You were saying, Mr Faraday.'

'Nothing really,' I said. 'Someone tried to kill me last night. I gathered he didn't want me on the case.'

Mrs Van Gimpel pursed up her lips and stared at me reflectively.

'You seem remarkably calm about it.'

I shrugged.

'It's my business,' I told her. 'You said someone as strong as King Kong and as hard as concrete might be involved.'

My client gurgled to herself somewhere down in the back of her throat.

'Those were your sentiments, so far as I recall.'

She put her head sideways, one eye on the gardener making mathematically precise cuts on the green turf below.

'You have something else to tell me.'

'That's right. There's a man called Freddie Ross in charge of your computer operations. He's giving print-outs to Adams' right-hand man, Eli Tombes. I can't prove it but that's my reading of it.'

Mrs Van Gimpel passed her tongue across her lips in a precise, old-maidish manner.

'Would you care to elaborate that, Mr Faraday?'

'I followed him to a small bar last night,' I said. 'When I was in your Headquarters building a girl there gave him a large brown envelope which he apparently needed for that evening. When he left I trailed him to this bar. He met Tombes there and gave him the computer print-outs. I know what they were because he took them out the envelope.'

Mrs Van Gimpel drew her breath in with a faint implosion of sound.

'You didn't make your presence known?'

I grinned.

'I'm a pro, Mrs Van Gimpel. I went quietly out into the rain without being seen. That was when someone tried to chop me. If he was one of Tombes' men my cover's blown anyway. I had no chance to check because he didn't stick around long enough for me to get the number of his heap.'

Mrs Van Gimpel's eyes were on the table top now. She looked as if she were going to cry. But instead she said in a very firm voice.

'And I suppose you don't want to go on with the case?'

'We haven't got a case yet,' I said.

Mrs Van Gimpel lifted her eyes to mine.

'You could keep the three thousand and we'll call it quits,' she said.

I shook my head.

'That's not my style. It's just that I thought you should know what's going on in your computer room. Maybe Adams is raking off a percentage of your business.'

Mrs Van Gimpel seemed dangerously calm though there were little spots of red burning on her cheeks.

'I'm deeply obliged to you, Mr Faraday. Just what do you intend to do?'

'Go on with the case,' I said. 'If the hitman wasn't connected with Tombes then he and Ross won't know I'm on to them. We'll just play things along for a while. I have one or two more angles to cover.'

The grey-haired woman gave a deep sigh and pulled herself up in the chair. I guessed then she kept her façade going by sheer will-power.

'I'm sorry the girls aren't here, Mr Faraday. You'd find them much more entertaining company.'

She lifted her head, a warning expression on her face. I slewed my chair slightly. Joseph and a girl in a dark dress were coming down the paving alongside the pool, wheeling a trolley on which the glancing sunlight struck shafts of brilliance from the shifting surfaces of silver and glass.

CHAPTER TWELVE

1

I got down to the end of the drive full of tea, toasted scones and no information round about five o'clock, the shadows carved long and heavy on the ground. There was a flash of white through the undergrowth as I rounded a curve and I reached for the Smith-Wesson. Then I recognised Joseph. He still wore the white drill suit and with his outfit, his grave deportment and his handsome, coffee-coloured features he looked as handsome and dignified as only that type of negro could look.

I took my unoccupied hand away from the inside of my jacket and slewed the Buick to a stop. Dust feathered across the driveway and Joseph brushed an imaginary speck off his lapel, displaying perfect teeth in a half-smile.

'I wondered if you'd mind doing me a favour, sir?'

'You can cut the Harriet Beecher Stowe crap,' I said. 'If you want a lift in to town why not say so? You must have a fleet of cars up here.'

Joseph's smile widened.

'Very well, Mr Faraday. The reason is simple. I have to go into town to pick up a vehicle which is being serviced for Mrs Van Gimpel. So I have a problem. Unless I strap an automobile to each foot.'

I stared at him, watching the shadows of tree-branches making little fretted lines across his finely-sculpted face. His hair was going grey around the temples, which added to his distinctive looks. I wondered why he wasted his time with a buttling job when he could have done so many other things. He was putting up a façade but he was obviously an educated man. Maybe he acted as a sort of informal business manager to Mrs Van Gimpel.

'You have a point,' I said. 'Get in.'

Joseph slid into the passenger seat and I engaged the gear, tooling the Buick on down to the private estate road. An inconspicuous blue truck drifted across the bonnet when we reached a cross-road, the uniformed man glancing with mock incuriosity at us, holding the plastic radio-telephone receiver to his ear. Our exit from the estate would be noted in a book somewhere, I figured.

Joseph eased back on the cushions with a grunt of satisfaction, the wind making little rippling patterns in his closely knit hair. I caught a glimpse of something bulky about his jacket which wasn't caused by muscle.

'You want to get a less conspicuous piece,' I said. 'Anyone can see that cannon a mile off.'

He stewed sidewise to look at me. He would have flushed if it had been technically possible.

'You may be right, Mr Faraday,' he said evenly. 'But I feel safer when I'm wearing it.'

I pulled the Buick over to avoid a station-wagon filled with blue-rinsed matrons that was veering dangerously close to us as it came from the opposite direction. I guessed they'd had a late lunch in L.A., followed by a few drinks and were just waltzing on back for an early cocktail party. It's a hard life for some, Faraday, I told myself.

'You're a funny sort of butler,' I said. 'Since when did that sort of staff need a firearms certificate?'

Joseph gave me a faint smile.

'I have various duties up at the house,' he said.

'So I gathered,' I told him. 'You hinted as much the last time we met.'

We were on a straight stretch of road now and I swivelled in my seat a little so that I could see him better.

'What's on your mind, Joseph?'

The tall man shrugged.

'Various things, Mr Faraday,' he said softly. 'But I'd like you to realise I'm on your side. I already told you if it's action you're after I'm ready to back you.'

I looked at him searchingly.

'Mrs Van Gimpel told you about last night?'

He nodded.

'That was bad, Mr Faraday. Like they say, two pistols are better than one.'

'Who said that?'

'Stendhal, I believe,' he said gravely.

I grinned.

'My, we got some culture in back of that white suit.'

He smiled too.

'Just so long as you remember, Mr Faraday.'

'I'll remember,' I told him.

I was slowing down now as we were approaching the main gate. The same man was on duty. He gave me a thumbs up sign as he recognised us and then the gate was swinging wide as he operated the button in his cubicle. I saw it close before we'd gone ten yards the other side. Joseph was silent until we joined the main-stem and were well on our way back into town.

'How do you read all this business, Mr Faraday?'

I gave him a sharp look, taking a second off from the fruit trucks and gasoline tankers I was dodging.

'What business?' I said.

He shrugged.

'Mrs Van Gimpel hired you to look out for the girls, Mr Faraday. You know that and I know it, because I had it from Mrs Van Gimpel herself. Why the shots?'

I waited until I'd drawn away from a scarlet coupé driven by a youth with wavy blond hair, who was executing some dangerous manoeuvres in the medium lane of the freeway.

'Your guess is as good as mine,' I said. 'But if you know that much you also know Valerie is mixing with some very ugly people.'

He shook his head like I'd given him a surprising answer.

'There's something more than that here, Mr Faraday,' he said slowly. 'I wish you'd give me a straight answer.'

'Maybe you're asking the wrong questions,' I said. 'You're in a position to give me more information than I can give you.'

'Perhaps,' he said wryly. 'It's at your disposal. So it's your turn to ask the questions.'

'It may take some while,' I told him.

He looked at the thickening traffic with disgust.

'It will take us an hour to get in at this rate,' he said. 'Ask away. I can't guarantee the answers but it will help to pass the time.'

2

Joseph's eyes flickered and he looked at me in disbelief. I was concentrating on sliding round the rear of a veering refrigerated truck and had to keep my eyes on the road. He let out his breath in a low whistle.

I had to repeat the question.

'There were some shots fired up on the estate too. Did you hear them?'

He shook his head.

'I don't know what you're talking about, Mr Faraday.'

'I understand there were shots heard at the edge of the estate one night,' I said cautiously.

I was concentrating on the steering but I could sense his eyes riveted on my face.

'Who told you that?' he asked quickly.

'It's restricted information,' I said. 'It's one of the things I'm currently trying to check out. I'm still waiting for the answer.'

Joseph shook his head again, his eyes worried. With his finely sculpted features he looked more than ever like some classical bronze statue.

'It's the first I've heard of it, Mr Faraday. It only increases my concern. I wish you'd take me into your confidence. I could help you a lot.'

I nodded.

'I don't doubt it. I'd like to let you in the picture but it may be too dangerous. I'll take a rain-check on your offer.'

Joseph made a low rumbling noise back in his throat.

'Someone tried to kill you last night,' he said in a subdued voice. 'Now you tell me there's been some shooting up at Spanish Oaks. It

98

gets more dangerous all the time.'

He turned back to me.

'When was this?'

I was still playing it cautiously.

'A week or two back.'

He gave me a glum look.

'That means Mrs Van Gimpel or the girls may be in danger.'

'Quite possibly,' I said.

'But that's not why you've been called in,' he said quickly.

'You know more than I do,' I told him. 'The whole thing may be tied up. I'd like you to keep your eyes open from now on.'

I took my right hand off the wheel and tapped his breast pocket.

'You know how to use that thing?'

Joseph smiled then.

'Try me, Mr Faraday. I could take the fuzz off a peach at thirty yards.'

'I'm fresh out of peaches at the moment,' I told him.

He didn't actually laugh this time but his face relaxed some.

'I'll remember what you said, Mr Faraday,' he added slowly. 'And thank you for your confidence. I'll keep a double check from now on. But I don't understand . . . With all the security we have up there . . .'

'Don't try to,' I said. 'Just keep your eyes peeled and I'd feel a lot happier.'

'And you will let me know if you want help

at the heavy end,' he said.

I smiled. I'd slackened speed now as we were drifting up to some lights.

'I'll do that,' I promised him.

'Fine, Mr Faraday.'

He put his hand over for a second and rested it gently on my shoulder.

'I'd appreciate it.'

He was looking sharply through the windshield now.

'If you'd be so kind as to turn right at the next intersection after the lights, you can let me off. It's about two blocks down.'

His eyes flicked to the amber hanging on its metal tubing high above the road.

'You can get back to the main-stem without turning around about half a mile farther on. Valparaiso Boulevard.'

'I'll remember,' I told him.

I turned right like he said when the lights changed, having to do some fancy steering, and tooled on down at slackened speed, searching for the place he wanted. I slid the Buick up on the cement concourse in front of one of the biggest and glossiest automobile showrooms I'd ever seen.

'You did say you were collecting one of the family's heaps?' I said.

Joseph grinned.

'I certainly did, Mr Faraday. No-one in their senses would pay their prices. They charge ten dollars just to wash your windshield.'

'Only the rich,' I said. 'Like you say, they're not always the most intelligent people.'

'You can say that again,' Joseph told me.

He slid out the passenger door quickly, turned to lean in.

'It's been a pleasant ride. And just call on me any time.'

'I'll do that,' I promised him.

I gunned on out, having to wait a couple of minutes at the edge of the apron to get in the traffic stream. I could see him striding down past the neon of the show-room windows to the servicing area. His big shoulders and athletic style looked purposeful, even dangerous at that moment. He would be a useful man to have in a roughhouse. I'd remember his offer and take it up if the time came.

His image dwindled in my mirror as I let in the gear. I found the intersection he was talking about and got back on the main-stem about where he'd said I would. I chewed over a few more possibilities in my mind on the way in but I didn't come up with anything that would have provided any useful ideas for Mickey Spillane, let alone a city police department.

I left it alone then, keeping my mind blank until I hit the junction I wanted. I have no trouble keeping my mind blank at the best of times. Even so I must have been half asleep. There was no-one around in the cubicle at the underground garage a couple of blocks from my office building, where I always stash the Buick.

I drifted across the acres of cement where naked bulbs cast shadowy obscurity beyond the steel and cement pillars that support the roof. I got in the slot that had my vehicle number chalked on a slate screwed to the wall and killed the motor. Silence crowded in, broken only by the distant dripping of a tap in a half-empty bucket in the area where people wash their cars down.

I started to get out the driving seat when a shadow crawled at the corner of my eye, coming round the concrete pillar next the near-side wing of the Buick. A hand as big as a ham-bone held the door effortlessly, half-open, half-shut. A fat man with cropped hair stood there. He had a genial face like a full moon and despite the heat he wore a belted white trench-coat of the sort I thought had gone out with Alan Ladd movies.

His eyes were genial behind horn-rimmed spectacles but his voice was as hard as a stick of Coney Island rock.

'Mr Faraday?'

'That's me,' I said, trying to make it convincing. The blued steel muzzle of the automatic in his other hand was suddenly lined up steadily on my gut. A small bead of sweat ran down the fat man's jovial face.

'We're going on a little trip, Mr Faraday.

Mr Tombes feels it's time you had a private chat.'

CHAPTER THIRTEEN

1

'Whoever he might be,' I said.

The fat man's gurgling laugh seemed to ooze and trickle round the pillars of the underground garage like storm-water running down a drain.

'You have quite a sense of humour, Mr Faraday. Let's go.'

'Sure,' I said. 'We can introduce ourselves later.'

The fat man slid into the passenger seat with astonishing swiftness. He held up the pistol reflectively, the dim light glinting on his glasses, like he was a professor and I some dumb student.

'I'm sure we're not going to need this, Mr Faraday.'

'I was hoping you'd say that,' I said.

He smiled thinly and slammed the passenger door. I fired the motor and let in the gear. We tooled slowly past the dim pillars and climbed the ramp that led eventually to street level. The fat man put the pistol back in his pocket. I kept my hands on the wheel and said nothing.

Something glinted down in the light of the dashboard. I caught a quick glimpse out the corner of my eye. The fat man had a big knife out. It vaguely reminded me of Spanish work; there were a lot of knives about like it in Southern California; sometimes sold in novelty shops at Spanish missions, museums and the like. I was sure this one had a retractable blade as there was no sheath the fat man could have taken it from.

The blade was very long and thin and sharp. He used it to clean his nails with, examining the results like he was in some high-class manicure parlour.

'I do not have to tell you, Mr Faraday, that I am equally adept with this instrument. We won't have any trouble.'

I shook my head.

'We won't have any trouble,' I repeated.

The fat man smiled greasily. He went on quietly working on his nails until we reached the street.

'Turn left and drive across town,' he said. 'I'll tell you when to stop.'

We drove for about half an hour. The fat man said nothing and I wasn't feeling very gabby myself. There was nothing to say really. I wondered whether Tombes just wanted a talk and if the trip was intended as a warning. Probably that because they might have left my heap in the garage otherwise. It was a fine point really and it wasn't a lot of comfort.

I had just turned at an intersection when the fat man reached over with a hard hand and took the Smith-Wesson from my holster.

'I wondered when you'd get around to it,' I said.

He grunted, examining the weapon as one professional to another.

'I knew you'd be too sensible to try anything, Mr Faraday. Besides, like all private dicks, you're curious. You'd want to know what Mr Tombes has to say. So you'd prefer to come anyway.'

I shrugged.

'You have a point, Mr . . . You do have a name.'

The fat man put the Smith-Wesson in his pocket.

'Call me Ferris. It's as good as any other.'

He suddenly tapped me on the shoulder.

'Pull over here.'

A red neon spelled out: BAR–DANCING in the dusk. We drove down the deserted lot. There was a black sedan waiting in the shadows underneath the trees, sparkling with chrome. A big man got out and came across the dim space between us. The fat man reached over and turned the ignition off. He took the key with him and got out the passenger door.

The two met about three yards away from the Buick and stood in low conversation for a couple of minutes. I could hear only a faint mumble; there wasn't even enough intelligible dialogue for me to get the gist of what they were saying. In the end they both came back to the Buick.

The big man was dressed in the same suit he'd been wearing when he met Ross. His white teeth looked like gravestones in the tight smile as he leaned down toward my driving window.

The headlights of the black sedan switched on, casting bars of yellow across his hard face. He put it up close to mine.

'This won't take long, Mr Faraday,' he said softly. 'We're going on a little trip.'

2

I turned off into the secondary road, the tyres biting as the Buick drummed up into the foothills. In the rear mirror I could see the fat man. He sat silent, like some character in a comic opera, the knife glinting as he precisely pared his nails. I'd felt the presence of the knife all the way up here but there was nothing I could do about it.

If they wanted to kill me they could do it any time. The fat man had the Smith-Wesson. Short of throwing myself out the vehicle at speed it was difficult to see what options were left me. Tombes hadn't been much help either.

He hadn't said a word since he'd gotten in the car. He sat with his big, well-kept hands still and relaxed in his lap.

His clothing came from an expensive tailor and there was a faint, elusive perfume about him that evidently emanated from some equally expensive aftershave.

I pulled the Buick round the next bend, changing down as the terrain became steeper. It was dark here, the wind gusting now and with hardly any traffic on the road. The only other vehicle was the big sedan which kept station about fifty yards behind, its headlights dipped. So far as I could see it held only the driver.

That made three; the odds were impossible even if I'd been armed. The wheelman of the sedan would be a pro too. I couldn't have held any one of them under the circumstances; not while I had to handle the driving. They'd made sure of that.

My thoughts were revolving like the ratchets of a pin-ball machine as the Buick jolted on uphill. I was short of ideas tonight. Not only about the opposition but on the details of the case. Such as it was. The more I thought about it the more blank and opaque it seemed. There had to be a key but it was for sure that I hadn't got access to it. Without it I couldn't unlock the door of the closet.

Which might or might not give me the information I was seeking. I gave it up then and concentrated on the driving. I must have been half-asleep but I snapped awake as Tombes straightened in his seat.

'This will do, Mr Faraday,' he said in his soft, almost languid voice.

I was tensing my belly muscles for something unpleasant and drastic when I realised he wanted me to turn again. The Buick's headlights, stencilled pallid and yellow against the dark undergrowth, steadied up on an anonymous black tarmac road; there was a white picket fence and a name-board but our progress was too quick and unexpected for me to make them out.

I could see the headlights of the sedan waltzing sedately in rear and for a second or two there was a blinding light in the mirror; he'd flicked his head-beams up momentarily. Perhaps for a given signal or just to make sure I wasn't trying anything fancy. I grinned wryly to myself in the mirror. As if I could.

Subtle as my change of expression was in the darkened interior, it hadn't been missed by Tombes. He had his left hand shoved down in his jacket pocket and I wondered for a moment if he had a gun in there. He could have taken me out any time during the journey, if so. My fingers trembled very slightly on the rim of the steering wheel and the bonnet of the Buick veered fractionally.

Tombes cleared his throat.

'Something amusing you, Mr Faraday?'

I nodded.

'Nothing that you would understand, Mr Tombes. Just life I guess.'

Tombes inclined his head. His eyes were still fastened to the front as though he could see things imprinted on the black tarmac of the roadway that were hidden from me.

'So you know me?'

I shrugged.

'I read the glossy social magazines.'

Tombes gave the rear mirror a dead smile. In the back the fat man stopped operating with the Spanish knife on his nails. His eyes, half-sunk in rolls of fat, were wide and staring now. He glanced casually from my reflection in the mirror to that of Tombes. Apparently he didn't see anything out of the way there because he dropped his glance after a moment and started work on his nails again.

The driveway seemed to go on for a long distance but I kept the Buick at a constant speed; the dark sedan ambling effortlessly along in our rear which told me there was a lot of power under the long bonnet; because we were still going steeply uphill. Tombes licked his lips, the smile faded from his face.

'You are either a very confident or a very foolish man, Mr Faraday.'

'So I've been told,' I said.

Tombes' hand made a sudden convulsive movement in the depths of his pocket, like he was having trouble controlling his emotions. I kept my eye on him from under closed lids, tensed to swing the wheel if he made any sudden movement. It didn't come and the tension slowly leaked out of the air in here.

The fat man made a heavy slithering noise on the cushions as he shifted position.

'Be polite, Mr Faraday,' he suggested in a low voice. 'It's far more sensible.'

'Thanks for the advice,' I said.

My knuckles showed white on the wheel as I pulled the Buick around the final curve. The heavy foliage lining the drive fell away and there was a large house with a white Palladian porch, ablaze with light and shining like a Christmas cake beneath the soft luminescence. I was so startled I almost missed the turn and drove the Buick over the edge of the smoothly shaved turf.

'Well, well,' I said. 'A social visit.'

I pulled the Buick up at the foot of a set of steps that wouldn't have been out of place at Franz Josef's palace in Vienna. Tombes bared his teeth and let out a faint sigh. He was enjoying himself now.

'What did you expect, Mr Faraday?'

His dead eyes swivelled to take me in full face.

'We are civilised people.'

I got out, the night wind fresh and cool on my face. The black sedan was coming up behind us. The headlights blinked out and it crunched to a halt some way farther down the concourse.

The big man went on up the steps without looking back. I followed on behind, taking them two at a time. Glancing around I could see the fat man several treads below. He was making heavy weather of it. I ignored him and followed the big man closely. We were on a sort of plateau now, with more well-tended acreage of grass; and a fine assortment of trees including a number of Spanish oaks that must have been hundreds of years old.

The house was really something as we got up closer. There seemed to be some sort of dance going on because I could hear the notes of an orchestra, thick and glutinous, coming out the open French windows of a vast room away to the right. As we went down a broad, stone-flagged walk beneath a pergola that bore heavy clusters of tropical plants I noticed the gleaming bonnets of parked automobiles way over to the left.

It was obvious that the road kept on going, following the slope of the hill, leading to the front entrance porch I'd already glimpsed from the foot of the steps. The fat man was close behind and I could hear his heavy breathing as we went steadily down the walk. I guessed he was pretty much out of condition, even for a fat character. All such details are useful to a man in my line of work. They might be doubly important tonight.

The pergola had given out now and we were

walking quietly across grass, the sound of the orchestra louder. There was a great glass conservatory down beyond the room where the music was. I could hear the buzz of conversation and the clink of glasses.

'What do you think of it, Mr Faraday?' Tombes said softly.

'It's all very nice,' I said. 'And entirely different from what I expected tonight.'

The big man looked at me with muddy eyes above the rat-trap mouth.

'You read too many comic books,' he said.

CHAPTER FOURTEEN

1

Tombes walked in over a black and white tiled marble floor without looking right or left. The stiff set of his back told me nothing. He might have been some business executive going in to a board meeting. An antique brass lantern fitted for electricity was burning up in the roof, suspended from a long chain set in a maze of rafters that had been picked out in blue and gold.

The light gleamed on the dark, almost sensuous sheen of fleshy leaves of shrubbery; and the bulbous, unhealthy-looking roots of tropical plants. Our footsteps echoed as we went down the big, glassed-in conservatory entrance that looked like something from another age.

'Wait here,' Tombes said tersely.

He left me underneath the lamp and walked on toward a wall of green forest that rose beyond a vast sheet of glass that arced up to the ceiling about forty feet above. He let himself in a sort of crystal lobby in a smooth, practised manner, like he'd been here hundreds of times before.

I looked around toward the entrance. The fat man in the raincoat was loitering in the open doorway. He glanced at me incuriously and then went away. I stayed where I was, grateful for the draught coming in. It was hot in here but I guessed it would be hotter where Tombes had gone. There was an unconscious joke lurking there somewhere but I was in no mood to work at it tonight.

I stayed put for what seemed like a long while. The faint music of the dance orchestra strayed in from time to time, probably due to changes in the direction of the wind outside; that and the ticking of a massive cased clock that stood against the far wall of the lobby were the only sounds.

It seemed like an hour but could in reality have been no more than ten minutes before Tombes came back. He gave me his tight-lipped smile, massive and durable-looking in his smartly tailored check suit. He motioned

113

with one hand over toward a banquette near the clock.

'If you'll take a seat, Mr Faraday, he won't keep you waiting long.'

'It's all right,' I told him. 'I'm not doing anything else this evening.'

His eyes seemed to flicker and smoulder for a moment; then he clenched his big fists and went on out, walking stiffly as if his legs were pegged like those of a marionette. I treated myself to one of my own tight-lipped smiles in the glass of the clock front and did like he said. I looked up at the faint click of the far door and saw that the lobby entrance to the grounds was deserted. I stayed put, lighting a cigarette and feathering out the smoke gratefully.

While I waited I reviewed a few more points in my mind. This was obviously Adams' house; it couldn't belong to anyone else. And a man like Tombes didn't defer to small fry. It had to be the big wheel himself. Which meant that he was pretty sure of himself.

I ran over what I knew about Mrs Van Gimpel's assignment; which wasn't much. I admired Adams' nerve. He'd come at the problem head on, so he figured he hadn't much to fear from me. That was also a valid and shrewd assessment. I was certain now he wanted to find out how much I knew. Which might call for a certain amount of caution and diplomacy on my part.

I hadn't approached Valerie Van Gimpel

direct; that was fortunate at this stage because she would have promptly passed the content of the interview on to Adams. I wondered idly whether the girl might be here tonight; or what the celebration might be for. For all I knew, with a man enjoying Adams' life-style he might well throw parties like this several times a week.

Yet it was rather a strange circumstance; to find a character with so much money and influence opting out and working in his greenhouse while the good time was going on somewhere else. I grinned at myself, stubbing out my cigarette on the heel of my shoe. I glanced at my watch. Incredibly, not much more than an hour had passed since the fat man had surprised me in the garage.

Still, I could have been lying out on a vacant lot somewhere instead of being an unsupervised guest up here; which meant that Adams wasn't sure about me and how much I knew. That was good to know. It would also be politic on my part to make him think I was in a stronger position than he thought. It was a fine line and the next hour would see whether I had been successful.

I put my cigarette stub back in the package and the match-stalk with it, my eyes fixed on the acres of glass around me, my senses dulled by the unexpected opulence of the surroundings. I was still sitting there as though hypnotised by the slow ticking of the clock when the far lobby door opened and a handsome blond man came through, giving me a ready smile.

2

I got up and went to meet him. He was wearing a white silk shirt and light grey trousers and perspiration glistened on his forehead. Behind him I could see a writhing jungle of trellised plants with here and there the blood red, gold or mauve splash of the blooms.

'I'm Mark Adams. But I expect you guessed that.'

The voice was low and cultured, not at all what I expected.

The tall man buttoned the cuffs of his sleeves. He dabbed at his forehead with an immaculate white handkerchief he took from his trouser pocket.

'I would ask you into the conservatory, Mr Faraday, but I'm sure you'd prefer somewhere cooler.'

He took his jacket and tie down from a brass hook set into a mahogany rack on the wall and led the way over the black and white marble concourse.

'You know anything about orchids, Mr Faraday?'

I shrugged.

116

'They're colourful, expensive and need a lot of heat. That and what you could get on the head of a pin.'

He gave me a glance of regret from his deep-set eyes.

'A pity, Mr Faraday. A man should have an interest. That is, apart from the humdrum business affairs of life.'

'You seem to have quite a few interests, Mr Adams,' I said.

He smiled again; a secret smile that seemed to die out at the corners of his mouth in some mysterious manner.

'Shall we go in here. This is my business room and we will be private. You'll not say no to a drink?'

He flung open a polished rosewood door at the far corner of the lobby and ushered me through.

'I don't like the rough stuff,' I told him while he was still closing the door. 'If you wanted to see me why not ring my office? I'm in the book.'

He looked startled and there was a spark of approval in his eyes as he stared at me. He crossed over to an old-fashioned desk which for some curious reason had a green baize top, making it look like a billiard table. Maybe it had something to do with his fragile plants; I was too angry to care at the moment. He sat down behind the desk, motioning me to a comfortable-looking eighteenth century leather chair in front. He raised his eyebrows.

'Rough stuff, Mr Faraday? Surely you are mistaken. I requested Mr Tombes to see if he could arrange this interview.'

I dropped into the chair, keeping my eyes steady on his face.

'It's your fat friend,' I said. 'He had a lethal-looking cannon on my gut for starters. Not to mention a toad-stabber.'

Adams smiled. He looked like a matinée idol for a moment, with his smooth blond hair and frank, open features and I could see why a nineteen-year-old girl like Valerie Van Gimpel could have gone overboard for such a character.

'You are talking about Lester, Mr Faraday. He means no harm. And I'm sure you're exaggerating.'

I shook my head.

'I'm not exaggerating, Mr Adams. It's not my style. But since we're here, let's talk. It will help to clear the air.'

Adams got up with a deprecating movement of his hands. He moved over to a set of crystal decanters and glasses that stood on a silver tray at the corner of his desk. It was very quiet in this elegantly panelled room with its copy of an Adam fireplace. The place was so solidly built that not even the faintest echo of the dance orchestra penetrated.

The blond man brought me back the drink in a long crystal goblet.

118

'You have no objection to Scotch?'

'Not at all.'

We drank in silence. He was studying me all the while he drank. I obviously puzzled him. He had the same effect on me, come to that. He re-seated himself at the desk, swilling his drink round moodily in his goblet.

'You appear to have a grievance, Mr Faraday.'

'I don't like getting shot at,' I said. 'I'm funny like that.'

A strange expression flickered across his face. He passed his tongue over even white teeth.

'I'm afraid I don't know what you're talking about.'

I shrugged.

'Someone tried to kill me last night. By firing three shots through the windshield of my heap. If my reflexes hadn't been good I wouldn't be here now.'

Adams had amazement on his face now. Either he was the best actor in the world or he was genuinely astonished. He got up and, as though trying to gain time, put on the dark blue silk tie and the jacket he'd carried in from the lobby. When he returned to his seat he was subtly transformed.

He put his fingers together on the blotter and stared at me reflectively.

'Would you believe me if I told you I had nothing to do with any shots fired at you last

119

night? Or any nonsense of that sort.'

'I might if it hadn't been for your fat friend,' I said.

Annoyance briefly flickered across Adams' strong features. He gave a faint sigh.

'I am a business man, Mr Faraday. I have vast and diverse interests.'

'So I've heard,' I said.

His eyes were focused somewhere over my shoulder now, like I wasn't there.

'One has to employ all sorts of people in large businesses.'

'So they tell me,' I said.

I took another sip at my drink. It was really good imported stuff. If I knew Adams he probably owned a distillery somewhere. Somewhere in Scotland, of course. They don't make real whisky anywhere else.

'You don't believe me, do you?' he said in an even voice.

I grinned.

'Strangely enough, I do, now that I've met you.'

He put his eyes down on the blotter, his whole figure relaxing.

'Thank you for something at least, Mr Faraday.'

'But you didn't ask me here for that,' I said.

He shook his head. His eyes were wide open now. I noticed for the first time that they were an extraordinary violet colour. They seemed to penetrate to the depths of one's soul. I

120

glimpsed for perhaps three seconds something of the power which had gained him control over a multi-million dollar empire. If the newspapers could be believed, of course. But then they always exaggerate. I took off a couple of million dollars just to balance things up.

'It has come to my notice, Mr Faraday,' he said in a very gentle voice, 'that you have been retained by Mrs Van Gimpel. Can you give me any indication as to why she requires your services?'

I shook my head.

'No way. I never give details of my clients' business to outsiders.'

Adams' eyelids flickered.

'Very laudable,' he murmured.

The eyes were wide and bright again.

'Not even for money.'

I shook my head.

'Especially not for money. I have a small business but it runs on integrity.'

There was the glint of something strange flickering in the eyes.

'Either you are a very foolish or a very noble man, Mr Faraday.'

I shook my head again.

'I never go in for extremes, Mr Adams. Nothing like that. I'm a cross between a sucker and a mule. It gets me into trouble sometimes.'

Adams reached up and brushed the back of his neck carefully with his disengaged hand.

'I can imagine,' he said drily. 'But it is an

121

attitude I respect. My regard for you has increased. I did not expect you to answer my question any other way but I had to put it.'

'I don't know where this is getting us,' I said.

The tall, blond man in the grey silk suit held up his hand suddenly.

'I'm coming to it, Mr Faraday. Please hear me out.'

'I'm listening,' I said.

He got up again in an abrupt way, his head on one side as though he were expecting something to break the profound silence of the room.

'Another drink, Mr Faraday. It is the least I can offer after the long drive and the inconvenience I have put you to.'

I let that one ride. I sat and watched him while he busied himself with the glasses. I had to admire his style though I wouldn't have admitted it openly. Truth was, I liked him more than I would have thought possible. As though he could read my thoughts he turned around.

'You've no doubt heard many stories about me, Mr Faraday.'

He was putting on his television charm smile now, which jarred on me a little.

'A few,' I admitted.

'Which put me in a bad light?'

'Perhaps,' I said.

I took the goblet from him. It was moist and cool to the touch and ice clinked agreeably in it. There seemed very little difference between the two poles of my case; Mrs Van Gimpel's luxurious life-style, won through legitimate business; and Mark Adams' even more opulent mansion, gained through non-legitimate activities. It was a dangerous philosophy and I decided I wouldn't buy it. Not even for a couple of superlative whiskies.

Adams had re-seated himself at the desk.

'As you know, newspapers and television producers exaggerate a great deal, Mr Faraday.'

'Perhaps,' I repeated.

He looked down at his finger-nails again.

'What I am trying to infer, Mr Faraday, is a little delicate and I am sure you won't take it the wrong way.'

'It would help if I knew what it was,' I said.

He made a little impatient movement with his shoulders but he was smiling faintly.

'It is extremely personal. I have a great interest in one of Mrs Van Gimpel's daughters. I would not like anything to interfere with that. Do I make myself clear?'

It seemed to have gotten very hot and close in the room now. I went on drinking my Scotch in silence. Adams was still staring at his finger-nails but there was a rigidity about his shoulders like a lot of power was coiled there, ready to strike.

'Precisely,' I said.

'What exactly does that mean, Mr Faraday?'

he said softly.

I got up from the chair, putting my empty glass down on the edge of the desk.

'Whatever you want it to mean, Mr Adams. Everything or nothing. I recognise your position. We could have had this conversation over the phone.'

He made a little gesture of disclaimer with his head.

'Not really, Mr Faraday. I wanted to know what sort of man you were. One can only discover that face to face.'

'Well, now you know,' I said.

He got up too.

'Now I know,' he repeated.

I started walking toward the door.

'Thanks for the drink,' I said.

'You're entirely welcome. And Mr Faraday . . .'

I turned at the door. His smile was open and sincere.

'Do please be careful. And remember what I said.'

'I'll remember,' I said.

I went on out and left him standing there in the silence and the elegance of the panelling. I could hear the dance-band again now. They were playing a jazzy thirties number, apparently in another world. My size nines slapped echoes from the marble as I went on down the lobby. The air outside seemed pretty cool after the hothouse atmosphere in there.

The fat man appeared from the depths of a colonnade that ran alongside the house before I'd gone a couple of yards. He still wore the white raincoat and the insincere smile. To my surprise he handed me the Smith-Wesson, butt first.

'I believe this is yours, Mr Faraday.'

'You know damn well it is,' I said.

I broke it open. I was surprised to see it was loaded. The fat man's smile became even wider.

'You see, we trust you, Mr Faraday,' he murmured.

I grinned.

'I wish I could return the compliment.'

I went on along the walk beneath the pergola, the bulk of the Smith-Wesson making a reassuring pressure against my shoulder muscles; the beat of the orchestra advancing and receding according to the strength of the wind. I got back down to the Buick to find the keys in the ignition. There was no sign of Tombes and the black sedan had gone. My brain started making like a fruit-machine before I'd gotten to the end of the private road.

CHAPTER FIFTEEN

1

It was around nine o'clock in the evening when I hit Freddie Ross' place. He lived in rear of a high-rise block in a bungalow-court apartment. They weren't really bungalows because they were two and even three storeys and he had a ground floor apartment on the far side. I parked the Buick at a corner of the lot shadowed by pepper trees and walked on over a crazy cement pathway that led in rear of the building.

I'd checked Ross out in the directory when I'd reached the edge of town. I walked on under an ornamental stone archway into the court which had some nice trees; a large open area of turf; and cobbled walkways, which were a mistake. They probably looked fine on the architect's drawings but they were hell on the feet.

Number 33 was at the far edge like I said and I walked into a small patio and buttoned the bell. Ross was sitting in the living room at an open window because a Japanese paper blind was pulled back and his worried face with the blinking eyes was staring at me.

'Who's there?'

He knew well enough because I was

standing directly under one of the ornamental lanterns that dotted the grounds in here. I leaned forward a little so that he could get a clearer view. There was a small bed of tropical flowers between the paving and his window and I was careful not to step on them because I could see he was a house-proud sort of guy.

'Oh, Mr Faraday.'

There was an alarmed bleat in the voice now.

'I do hope there's nothing wrong with our computer programming.'

I smiled.

'Nothing like that, Dr Ross. I'd just like to have a quick word with you.'

He pulled the blind a little higher.

'Of course.'

'Not here,' I said gently. 'It would help if I could come in.'

He suddenly pulled himself together.

'Oh, I'm so sorry. It's just that I don't get many visitors. I won't be a moment.'

I heard a clattering noise as he dropped the blind and a few moments later bolts and catches were drawn back on the door. They didn't have as much security when Edmond Dantes arrived at the Chateau d'If.

Ross was wearing an open-neck blue shirt with a white wool waistcoat over it and his sandy hair was rumpled like he'd just come from his bed. But he held a scratch-pad in his hand and from the ink-stains on his fingers

127

I guessed he'd been engaged in some calculations.

His thin smear of mustache looked like the stain of blood beneath the subdued lighting of the wall fixture over his head. He showed me into the small, cramped hall which was lined with tall piles of cardboard boxes. From the printed labels I guessed they contained equipment; others held technical magazines and printed data to do with computer technology.

Ross smiled apologetically, closing the door behind us and locking and bolting it again.

'I guess all bachelors get a little untidy living alone.'

'Sure,' I said. 'I'm a bachelor myself.'

He nodded, putting the scratch-pad down on top of the nearest pile of boxes.

'Come on in, Mr Faraday. I was just about to have some coffee. You'd like some?'

'Fine,' I said.

I followed him into a crowded living room which nevertheless contained some very good pieces of antique furniture; an elaborate hi-fi outfit which seemed to take up one wall. Above it were rack after rack of record albums, mostly of classical music. Dr Ross motioned me to an upholstered easy chair which stood the far side of the natural stone fireplace facing his own in front of the window.

The Japanese paper blind stirred slightly in the night breeze, bringing with it a faint aroma of tropical flowers mingled with gasoline fumes.

'I won't be a moment.'

He went out and through the half-open door I could see a miniature kitchen, gleaming with chrome and steel-plated gadgets. That figured too. I wondered how much Ross made with the San Rosario set-up. It must have been a nice living. I mentally queried why he would need to supplement it by selling material to Mark Adams. I'd maybe find out if I asked him the right questions.

He didn't strike me as exactly being too bright so far as the ordinary modes of living went. But then many scientists weren't. Some of the most famous in the world had been downright idiots so far as their personal lives were concerned. Just like the rest of us, in fact. I grinned to myself at the thought and waited for Ross to return.

The room lights dimmed slightly then. I guessed he'd switched on some form of heavy-duty stove to make the coffee. He came back and lounged in the half-open doorway, an awkward, ungainly figure, still blinking beneath the pebble glasses. Despite the differences in physique he reminded me briefly of the fat man and the way he looked from beneath his horn-rims. But the analogy ended there.

Ross shuffled his feet, humming tunelessly to himself.

'The coffee won't be a moment,' he mumbled.

He rubbed his hands with a thin rasping sound.

'Then I'm entirely at your disposal.'

2

Sweat glistened on Ross' face and in among the roots of his sandy hair. He moved his chair a little closer to the Japanese paper blind as though grateful for the slight wind which came in through the open window.

I sipped my coffee cautiously. It wasn't as good as Stella makes but then I hadn't expected it to be. But at the same time it was extremely good for a bachelor living on his own like Ross. He licked his lips with a bluish tongue and looked at me hesitantly like our interview was going to be an ordeal.

I wasn't in any particular hurry to begin and I wanted to choose my words with care. Ross could give me a valuable lead if I handled him properly. He seemed remarkably naïve away from his technical apparatus but that could have been a façade.

'I must say I was surprised at your visit, Mr Faraday.'

I shrugged.

'I don't see why, doctor. I find it's often better to chat with personnel away from the office atmosphere. They have more time, for one thing.'

He nodded portentously like I'd said something profound.

'I'd like a little amplification on procedures,' I went on. 'We can take your programming operations as read.'

Ross looked at me approvingly.

'Thank you, Mr Faraday. No doubt you've seen the material I've circulated throughout all offices.'

I nodded. I picked up the ball he'd thrown me and sent it back.

'Most definitely,' I said. 'They were a model of their kind.'

Ross flushed slightly and shifted to a more comfortable position in his chair.

'I can see we'll get on, Mr Faraday.'

'One can't always judge a man in business surroundings,' I said.

Ross flushed again.

'I'm afraid I may have given you a bad impression when first we met. I was rather harassed and on edge.'

'That's all right,' I said. 'The 4FT.'

Ross smiled thinly, his eyes shy and withdrawn beneath the thick pebble lenses of his glasses.

'I'd like to talk about security now,' I said. 'What specific material and what sort of material goes out the Control Room.'

Ross shook his head.

131

'That's simple, Mr Faraday. Nothing without company authorisation. There are only two people authorised to take documents out. Myself, of course; and my Deputy Director.'

He beamed.

'That way security is maintained. It was something Mrs Van Gimpel insisted on. And I agree with her one hundred per cent.'

'And what sort of people would you supply material to,' I said. 'Aside from our own organisation.'

'Businesses associated with us, naturally,' Ross said. 'And certain companies who use our computer facilities under contract. That's a very valuable part of our revenue, of course.'

'Quite,' I told him.

This might be easier than I figured. I just let him keep on talking. Like all enthusiasts, once he got on to his own subject there was no holding him.

'For example,' he said. 'I took a long print-out for a firm only last night. I handed the material to Mr Keefer, who's a director of Allied Zinc, one of our contracted companies.'

He beamed.

'I can give you a list of all the companies with whom we deal in this way. I have it right here.'

'I'd like it,' I said.

He rummaged around in a leather briefcase on the table in front of him, came up with two stapled photo-copy sheets of immaculately typed data. I put them down at my side; I'd study them at my leisure. I saw the list was alphabetical, with Allied Zinc at the top.

'What is this Mr Keefer like,' I said. 'I may know him.'

Ross seemed absolutely unconscious of the import of my questions.

'A very tall, powerfully built man, with silver hair. He occasionally comes into the San Rosario H.Q. But I sometimes meet him outside to pass stuff over, when it's more convenient to him.'

I nodded. His description of Keefer exactly fitted Tombes. Maybe Dr Ross was as innocent as he made out. Nobody could be that dumb unless it was absolutely inbred. I looked at Ross again. I guessed it was inbred, all right. The only thing that interested him in the world —apart from music, perhaps—was computers.

It was Ross' turn to quiz me. He leaned back, his coffee cup in his right hand, his left idly stirring the spoon. His eyes glistened benevolently behind the glasses, his head slightly turned to get the benefit of the breeze gently agitating the Japanese blind.

'You have done well, Mr Faraday, if I may say so, to inspire such confidence in Mrs Van Gimpel.'

I made a deprecating movement of my shoulders, nuzzling into my coffee again. I didn't reply and Ross tried again, his eyes watchful now, fixed on my face.

'I meant merely that the lady is difficult to know. She occasionally seems very hard to her employees. Though she spends a great deal of time up at Spanish Oaks and hardly ever appears at the San Rosario Building, she seems to know everything that is going on.'

He stopped stirring and waved his left hand languidly.

'Even to the most subtle nuances of office gossip . . .'

He left the sentence hanging in the air. I didn't help him any, just looked pointedly at my empty cup.

'Glad you liked it, Mr Faraday. Have another.'

I reached over and poured myself a cup from the glazed earthenware pot, refreshed his own. There was a heavy silence between us. I decided to help him this time.

'Mrs Van Gimpel is a remarkable woman,' I said.

He nodded.

'Considering she has had such a tragic life, it's doubly impressive that she's been able to build such a successful business empire.'

I frowned at him over the rim of my coffee cup.

'You mean the two girls? The difficulties of a widow bringing them up on her own?'

He shook his head.

'You mean to say you don't know?'

His eyes narrowed.

'I'm not in Mrs Van Gimpel's confidence to that extent,' I said.

'I thought everyone in San Rosario knew that story,' he said.

Then his face cleared.

'But you are a fairly new boy, Mr Faraday. And you come from the East.'

He leaned forward in his chair like the business was confidential.

'I was referring to Mrs Van Gimpel's husband. He died under very mysterious circumstances about fifteen years ago. Some people say he was murdered.'

I put my cup down on the saucer with a brittle chinking in the silence of the room.

'How did he die, Dr Ross?' I said.

The eyes were clouded behind the pebble lenses.

'He fell off a bridge at a tourist scenic spot up in one of the canyons, Mr Faraday. But witnesses in the gorge below said there were two people up there. He was thrown off, according to some.'

'Interesting,' I said slowly.

Ross nodded.

'Very interesting. It was a tragic business. The family were stricken. But Mrs Van Gimpel, as I said, is a very determined woman. She used her husband's money wisely. And in fifteen years she has built up a multi-national corporation, almost single-handed.'

'With the aid of her husband's money,' I said.

Ross gave a thin smile.

'Money does help, Mr Faraday.'

'You're right there,' I said. 'I'd like to ask you one or two more questions.'

'Fire away,' Ross said.

I put my cup down, bent to locate the saucer. Ross gave a faint choking sound then, like he was clearing his throat. The cup trembled in his lap and fell over, staining his trousers. I looked at him sharply. He was keeling sidewise, his eyes closed behind the glasses. A thin trickle of glutinous black blood ran out the corner of his mouth.

I got to my feet just in time to see the strangely patterned knife-blade going back through the slit in the Japanese paper blind. It was quite a moment and my reflexes were slow. I reached for the Smith-Wesson as Ross hit the floor with a crash, a great scarlet stain spreading on the back of his white wool waistcoat. He was already dead by then.

I flailed with the pistol barrel through the blind into the darkness beyond, heard someone grunt. Already feet were scraping on the cobbles of the courtyard. I got over to the switch and doused the lights. I was making too good a target in here. I'd recognised the knife all right. Either these people were careless or they had no fear of reprisals. I rolled up the blind and went out through the open window, being careful not to land in the flower bed.

I sprinted down the concourse beneath the pallid glare of the lamps. Nothing moved except for the shaking of the foliage in the night wind. A car gunned up in the next block as I got to the entrance of the office building.

I put the Smith-Wesson back in my holster then. I went back down toward Ross' place. There might be something in his papers that could be helpful. It was something I had to try. I hadn't gone ten yards when there was the sound of music and people started spilling out one of the bungalow court apartments next to Ross' place.

I turned on my heel then and went away fast, walking on the balls of my feet. Ross would be missed at San Rosario tomorrow morning but as he'd locked the front door it might be a day or two before he was found. Which would give me some time. There was my cup and saucer, covered with my prints, of course. And I may have been seen going in. I'd meet that when I had to. I didn't intend to tell Mrs Van Gimpel what had happened for the moment. Only Stella would know; and the man who'd shoved the knife-blade in Ross' back.

Someone might be curious about the open window and the drawn blind. But I felt I might count on half a day before anything popped. I got back in the Buick and drove around the block to find a pay-phone and give Stella the good news.

CHAPTER SIXTEEN

1

It was close again this morning, despite the imminence of rain, and I was glad to get into the cool, air-conditioned interior of the Reference Library. They'd only been open a couple of minutes and a tall ash-blonde with a rangy walk was flustered and had to get the keys to open up their archives for the material I wanted. There was a No Smoking sign on the wall but I seemed to be their first customer of the day and I had the big viewing area to myself.

The girl, whose name was Peggy Clifford, according to the small blue and white plaque pinned to the front of her dress, came back in the end with the three cassettes of micro-film I'd requested. She also brought me a plastic carton of coffee and put it down on the table at my elbow.

'Be my guest, Mr Faraday.'

'I could get to like it here,' I said.

I could feel her smile burning my shoulder blades even as she got to the door. She turned in the entrance.

'You know how to work the thing, Mr Faraday?'

'I think so,' I said. 'If I want any help I'll

shout.'

She smiled again.

'I'll be just across the corridor,' she promised.

She went on out, the pneumatically-operated door hissing gently to behind her and left me alone with the air-conditioning, the filtered sunlight from the high windows and the blank silence ensured by the heavy plate glass and double glazing. I took the plastic top off the coffee and tasted it. It was already sugared and wasn't half as bad as I'd figured. I decided I'd bring the girl back a box of chocolates before she closed this evening. She'd been more helpful than anyone had a right to expect.

I switched on the machine, which she'd already loaded with the first cassette. The front page of *The Examiner* blinked into focus on the small TV-type screen in front of me, pin sharp in every detail; there was another control to bring up the fine stuff into big close-up but I didn't need that for the moment. I was looking for headlines.

There were plenty of them and I'd worked through my cup of coffee; six months of murder, mayhem and international disasters; to say nothing of an hour of my time before I struck gold. There were half a dozen or so other researchers in by then but they weren't making any more noise than a crowd of argumentative limpets so they didn't bother me any.

For some reason I must have overshot a couple of issues because a stop-press item first drew the story to my attention. I turned back; there was a front-page streamer which said: HEIR TO VAN GIMPEL MILLIONS PLUNGES TO DEATH. I turned to page three like they said and digested the story in silence.

There were pictures of Van Gimpel himself; the widow, looking considerably more chic and obviously younger than now; and the two bereaved children, golden-haired tots who stared wide-eyed out of the newsprint. I went down the columns, forgetting the measured pacing of the big clock that hung high up on the wall, its gilded pendulum, swinging six feet below it, making a glittering arc in the sunlight. It reminded me of the atmosphere in the conservatory lobby up at Adams' house.

The stories roughly confirmed what Ross had told me. Max Van Gimpel had been on the bridge and had fallen five hundred feet to the floor of the gorge at a place called San Antonio Gap. He'd been killed instantly, of course. The interesting thing was the wide diversity of opinion among spectators.

There had been nobody else on the bridge at the time, so far as was known, though at least three people had testified to seeing a tall man who appeared to be arguing with the millionaire before he went over. His own roadster was found parked back in the trees about a hundred yards from the bridge entrance. At least two witnesses spoke of seeing a black sedan driving off. But as everyone who'd seen anything had been at the bottom of the gorge it wasn't too difficult to work out some of the problems for the authorities.

The autopsy had revealed nothing but what one would expect; Max Van Gimpel had broken every bone in his body in the fall and had died instantly. There were no other marks or signs of any sort of attack or violence before he went over; or at least, anything that could be scientifically identifiable after such a fall.

I turned to the other autopsy reports which followed but the stuff was merely a repetition of the earlier stories; I already knew no-one had come up with anything in the intervening fifteen years so I didn't waste my time with later issues.

I switched off the machine in the end and sat staring at the patterns the sunlight was making on the opposite wall. The verdict had been an open one and the coroner had drawn the attention of the highway authorities to the dangerously low rail on the bridge; there was another short story on the same page to say the barrier was shortly to be heightened.

I took the cassettes back to the desk but there was another girl on duty. I asked her for copies of the relevant stories I wanted and she said they'd be ready in half an hour. So I went out, bought a box of candies like I'd promised and found a coffee shop where I knocked my thoughts around for a while.

Someone had left a copy of today's *Examiner* on the seat opposite and I riffled through it while I ate my sandwich. There was nothing in the stop-press about the Ross kill so I guessed he hadn't been found. It was time to go back to the Library by then so I went across, collected my photocopies and paid for them.

The tall blonde number still wasn't around so I wrote her name on the wrapped package and left it with the second girl. She raised her eyebrows and I could feel her curiosity all the way to the main entrance. It's something to do with the new type of librarian they have these days. They don't come any better. And they're intelligent too.

2

Stella put one well-groomed finger-nail on the top photo-copy and frowned at it.

'Did he fall or was he pushed?' she said.

I shrugged. 'A classic question. My vote goes to pushed.'

'You may be right,' Stella said.

She cupped her chin in her hands and read on in silence for a few minutes. I set fire to a cigarette and studied the cracks in the ceiling. They didn't help me any but at least they didn't detract from my knowledge of the case; which was more or less zero.

Stella finished up at last and rose to her feet. She went over to the alcove in silence and I heard the snick of the percolator going on. The sound reminded me of something. I got the envelope out my pocket and removed the slug I'd taken from the tree up at Spanish Oaks. Then I got the second slug I'd dug out the Buick's upholstery before I drove into town this morning.

It had taken me half an hour to find it and I wouldn't have then except it had embedded itself in a wooden upright which held the squab. Stella came over and stared down at me. I put the two slugs together and studied them.

'Same type of pistol?' Stella said.

I nodded.

'Maybe. Both small calibre stuff. There's a good chance they may match.'

Stella put her head on one side and looked at me with very blue eyes.

'So you want ballistics?'

'It would help,' I said. 'My finances don't run to laboratories. But I'm sure you have a friend in Police H.Q. downtown.'

Stella smiled, passing a pink tongue over full lips.

'I'm sure I have,' she said softly.

She picked up the two slugs quickly, put

143

them back in the envelope and took them over to her desk.

'We need a fresh envelope before you take them to the lab,' I said. 'My name's not to come in to it.'

'You took the words right out of my mouth,' Stella said.

There was just the faintest hint of reproach in her voice. She went over to the alcove again and put the coffee down on my blotter.

'You seem a little touchy this morning, Mike.'

'It's just the case,' I said. 'The usual boring routine. Like I said, Ross got dead last night. Right in front of my eyes. While I sat there drinking coffee like now.'

Stella didn't say anything. She went back to the alcove to collect her own cup. She didn't speak again until she'd taken the first sip, added a little more sugar.

'You want to talk about it?'

I shrugged.

'Nothing much to tell. I believed Adams when he said he had nothing to do with those shots. So why would he send Ferris to take out Ross only a couple of hours afterward?'

Stella wrinkled up her nose. It didn't affect her beauty any.

'How do you know it was the fat man?'

'Because I recognised the knife,' I said. 'It's the same one he uses to trim his nails.'

Stella raised her eyebrows.

144

'You mean Ross got stabbed?'

I nodded.

'Right through a Japanese paper blind as we sat talking. Either Adams didn't know about it and Ferris—or Lester—was acting on his own. Unless he was nuts. That figures too.'

Stella stirred her coffee gently, her eyes on my face.

'Perhaps Tombes wanted Ross dead.'

'It hadn't escaped my notice, honey,' I said.

'Maybe Tombes sent Ferris to tail you,' Stella persevered. 'And he simply acted on his own, without instructions. Which could mean Ross had some information they didn't want you to get.'

I stared at her for a long moment. The more I thought about it the more I felt she'd got something.

'That could be it,' I said. 'There's something staring me in the face about this case and I can't see it.'

Stella put up a hand to pat into place a strand of hair on her immaculate coiffure.

'Adams doesn't really care about you, Mike. You can't harm him. And you haven't anything on him. All he was concerned about was that you didn't louse up his romance.'

'Keep on talking,' I said. 'I don't want to miss a syllable.'

Stella smiled faintly. It made the room even lighter if anything.

'Supposing Ferris shot at you outside that

bar. He was keeping tabs on Tombes.'

I wasn't so sure about that.

'It's possible,' I admitted. 'But unlikely. It was light stuff, like I said. Ferris carried a big cannon.'

Stella glanced over toward the envelope on her desk.

'We shall know soon enough,' she said. 'I'll shut up shop for an hour and ask my friend to phone me here when he has something. We may hear by late afternoon.'

It was my turn to raise my eyebrows.

'As soon as that?'

Stella looked reflectively at the surface of her coffee cup.

'My friends don't hang around when it comes to passing out favours,' she said.

'I can imagine,' I told her.

It may have been my imagination, but I fancied I saw a faint red burning on Stella's cheeks beneath the tan. She got up quickly and went over to fetch me a second cup.

She stood and watched me as I started to drink it.

'What will you be doing?' she said. 'Just for the record.'

I stared toward the shimmering haze of smog and automobile fumes over the distant boulevard.

'I'll just sit here for a bit,' I said. 'Mrs Van Gimpel's case is starting to bite. I've had a bad shock to my system.'

'I'll get you a good bottle of nerve tonic on my way back in,' Stella promised.

She was still smiling when she left for the lab.

CHAPTER SEVENTEEN

1

There was a light rain starring the windshield as I pulled in to the parking lot in front of the San Rosario set-up. I glanced at my watch. It was only a quarter of five so there was plenty of time. I hadn't brought a raincoat this afternoon so I stepped it out fairly smartly, heading across the boulevard to the shelter of an Old Englishe-type tea-shop. I'd passed it before so I knew they had a pay-booth.

Stella came on almost as soon as the phone started ringing so I guessed she'd been waiting for my call.

'You hit the jackpot, Mike. The riflings on those two slugs matched up.'

'Thank your contact for me,' I said.

Stella made a low gurgling noise way down in her throat.

'He's buying me lunch tomorrow,' she said.

'Bully for him,' I told her.

I stared at the graffiti on the booth wall, not registering it, tossing the new information

147

around, trying to make it fit in a place where the existing pattern wouldn't go.

'So whoever fired the shots up at Mrs Van Gimpel's also fired at you,' Stella said.

'You're sharp this afternoon,' I said.

Stella ignored that. I should have done the same in her place.

'What does it mean, Mike?'

'Maybe the same person who doesn't like Valerie Van Gimpel doesn't like me,' I said. 'Who knows? I'm waiting to see her now, incidentally.'

'I thought you'd gone over to shoot some pool at your senior citizens' club,' Stella said.

I made a clicking noise with my tongue.

'You're getting touchy, honey,' I said. 'It's a bad sign.'

'It's the weather,' Stella said. 'Is it raining your end?'

'Just beginning. Any more information on those slugs?'

'They were fired from a Walther PPK,' Stella said.

'Fairly light stuff, like I figured,' I said. 'Magazine-loading and easily concealed. Doesn't tell us a lot but at least it's nice to know.'

I thanked her again and replaced the phone. I lit a cigarette and put the spent match-stalk back in the box. It was raining nicely now and the details of the boulevard outside were beginning to get blurred. I waited until there was a lull in the traffic and sprinted back to the Buick. I got behind the wheel and worked away at what Stella had told me.

I wondered if Tombes and his hit-man were playing some game of their own. Perhaps the fat boy had been hidden in the garden that night and had tried to take Adams out. It was a possibility but it still didn't explain how he had left the estate without being seen by the guard. Or how he'd got in come to that. I worried on at it for the duration of a couple of cigarettes but there was some intractable improbability at the heart of the whole mess that eluded me.

It was a quarter after five before the girl showed and I almost missed her. She was wearing a white slicker with a pixie hood that shielded her face but I'd already checked out her heap and I got across there just as she was putting the key in the driving door.

'Well, well. Mr Faraday, isn't it?'

The handsomely insolent face framed beneath the blonde hair still had the sullen look but somehow Valerie Van Gimpel appeared a good deal more attractive and forthcoming this afternoon.

'Always has been,' I said. 'I'd like a word with you if you're not in too much of a hurry.'

The girl stood as though in thought, her right hand still on the door latch. She shook her head.

'I have all the time in the world, Mr Faraday. But it's somewhat damp here and a

149

little early for bars.'

'So they tell me,' I said. 'There's a tea-room almost opposite. I take it you've no objection to tea?'

There was amusement on the flawless features now. When time and the problems of the world had stamped a little more character and compassion into them, Valerie Van Gimpel would possess a unique sort of beauty. I could see why a man like Mark Adams would be so attracted. She ran her tongue round full lips.

'No, I've no objection to tea.'

She shot me a glance from beneath the deep-fitting hood as she re-locked the driving door of the stone-coloured convertible.

'You've been talking to my sister, Mr Faraday.'

'I've been talking to everyone,' I said.

She put up one hand to push back some straying strands of hair from her eyes.

'You talk to too many people, Mr Faraday. It can be unhealthy in a town like L.A.'

I stared at her for a moment as we went down the parking lot together. A great mass of people were drifting out the San Rosario Building now and the traffic was thickening up nicely.

'Is that meant to be a warning, Miss Van Gimpel?'

She shook her head.

'Just friendly advice.'

'Taken in the same spirit,' I said, as we waited for a stop light so that we could cross the boulevard. She shot me a mischievous glance.

'I'm surprised you recognised me with my clothes on.'

'I'd recognise you anywhere,' I said. 'Even with a screen of bushes between us.'

She gave me a pouting look, half-defiant, half-amused.

'It should be an interesting conversation, Mr Faraday.'

'I'll try to make it so,' I told her.

2

The smoke from my cigarette went up in a hazy blue spiral toward the fretted ceiling of the tea-shop. On the boulevard outside figures went by in the downpour like dimly-glimpsed creatures in an aquarium. The girl sat opposite me, slightly tensed, as we waited for our order. She wore a low-cut blouse of some thin white material that clung to her full figure.

The place was filling up because of the weather and we had managed to find a corner booth for two so we could talk privately. I was in no hurry to begin and the girl herself didn't seem curious.

I'd offered her a cigarette but she'd preferred to smoke her own, selecting a

Turkish from a silver case she produced from a small shoulder bag. It would have been silver, of course. It might even have been a product of the San Rosario outfit for all I knew.

I glanced at the indistinct bulk of their building through the sheeting rain. The cafe was one of those places where they serve afternoon tea until eight in the evening so we had plenty of time.

'What do you do over there?'

I was passing time until the waitress had come and gone and she knew it.

'Mother must surely have briefed you adequately, Mr Faraday. I can't believe she sent you out without boning you up on both my good and bad habits.'

I grinned faintly through the smoke.

'I'd rather have it from your own lips.'

She shrugged.

'Mother has the idea that I'll run the whole shoot one day. So I'm going through the mill.'

'Do you like it?' I said.

She shrugged again.

'Moderately interesting. The money's all right. Mother makes it up with a private allowance.'

The green eyes flashed.

'It saves jealousy among the other employees.'

'You said you'll be running the place,' I said. 'What about Erica?'

The face was turned down toward her plate

now, half hidden in the cloud of golden hair.

'It goes without saying that Erica will be there too. Senior partner, of course. She's got a legal degree, but I expect you know that. She's with a partnership here in L.A., specialising in company law and corporation tax for when she takes over. She'll run the business side and I'm supposed to come up with the marketing ideas.'

'It sounds a golden future,' I said.

She shifted uneasily in her seat as though I'd said something untoward.

'It's all right if you like that sort of thing.'

'It's money,' I said. 'Don't you like money?'

The eyes were half-closed against the cigarette smoke, the expression again sullen.

'Oh, that. I've heard nothing but that since my childhood.'

'You have all the contempt of a rich person for ready cash,' I said. 'It's only the rich who can afford such attitudes.'

She gave me a genuine smile then. She looked really beautiful at that moment. There were a good many similarities between the two sisters except that the elder had long passed the insolent stage.

'You may be right, Mr Faraday. But don't give up hope. I could grow out of it as the years roll by.'

'You will,' I said.

The buxom waitress in the pink gingham was back at the table now, rattling around briskly with cutlery, stoneware pots and plates of cakes. She put the stuff down as efficiently as a croupier dealing a deck of cards and withdrew in thirty seconds flat. With the place filling up like that I guess she'd be losing hours on the day if she couldn't keep up the turnover. We were on the scones and buttered toast and the girl was pouring the tea with skilful and practised movements before she spoke again.

'Did mother ask you to give me a grilling, Mr Faraday?'

I grinned.

'Don't exaggerate, Miss Van Gimpel. I haven't asked you one question yet.'

She put her hand up to cradle the side of her head. 'You will, Mr Faraday. And my name's Valerie.'

'I'm honoured,' I said. 'All right, Valerie. And the name's Mike.'

She smiled too.

'I'm still waiting for the questions, Mr Faraday.'

'I'll try not to disappoint you,' I said.

'Supposing I make it easier for you,' she said. 'I'm keen on Mark Adams, like you've been told. We've been going around for some while.'

She broke off to give me a defiant look over her teacup.

'Not that it's any business of yours.'

She reached out for another piece of toast,

154

wiping her fingers fastidiously on a paper napkin.

'Mr Adams is a bad man, Mr Faraday, or didn't you know. Aren't you frightened at mother's assignment?'

'Terrified,' I said.

I picked up my cup and tasted the tea. It was pretty good stuff if you liked that sort of thing. I can take it or leave it. This afternoon I decided to take it.

The girl put her head on one side and studied me in silence for a moment or two.

'I must admit you have style, Mr Faraday. But Mark Adams will cut you down to size.'

'I had a chat with him last night,' I said.

There was surprise in the girl's eyes now. It was genuine. There was no mistaking it.

'Don't tell me you don't know.'

She shook her head, the sullen look back again.

'He didn't mention it when we spoke on the phone this morning. What happened?'

'Nothing very much,' I said. 'I didn't make him any promises, if that's what you mean.'

She put her cup down with a brittle chinking noise. I noticed her fingers were trembling slightly.

'About what, Mike?'

'About the situation,' I said.

I leaned forward across the table. The green eyes were smoky now and I couldn't read their expression.

'Look,' I said. 'I'm trying to be kind to you. You're mixing in things of which you know nothing. A little girl like you would soon be in way over her head.'

Valerie Van Gimpel raised her eyes, a wry, almost resigned expression on her face.

'Don't meddle in things you know nothing about, Mr Faraday. Believe me, I'm sure you mean no harm. But you might be making things very much worse.'

I stubbed out the butt of my cigarette on the torso of a nude girl who was prancing around the edge of the ash tray in the centre of the table. I didn't know they had such things in Old Englishe tea-shops but I guessed the proprietors here ought to know.

'What things?' I persisted.

The girl had a stubborn set to her chin.

'Mark Adams is a very fine person. There are all sorts of stupid stories around about him. He's explained everything to me. You and mother are on the wrong tack.'

She stubbed out her own cigarette with a desperate gesture, her face disfigured and distorted with suppressed passion. I remembered what Erica had told me then. This was a very immature girl who would be easily led, particularly by someone like Adams.

'Just leave us alone, Mr Faraday.'

She got up quickly and went on out, walking with her head held high, heads turning as she walked. It seemed like she felt she might already have said too much. It was about what I figured but I was sorry she hadn't stayed because I might have gotten something out of her in another quarter of an hour.

I sat on and smoked another cigarette, finishing up the toast and the cakes, ordering another pot of tea to go with them, while I waited for the rain to clear.

CHAPTER EIGHTEEN

1

It was dusk when I got back to the office. Stella had obviously been gone a long time but there was a note on my desk. It asked me to ring her but when I dialled the number there was no reply. I frowned at my reflection in the dark surface of the window. It was about what I figured. Either she hadn't yet reached home or she'd gone out again.

I sat down at the desk and set fire to a cigarette. The office had a stale, unlived-in smell now. It was something I'd noticed at night. No matter how much air came in during the day or how hard the fan worked, the moment things shut down for the night it seemed like the place had been empty for years. It probably had something to do with the melancholy public buildings seem to exude

157

after dark.

Neons were making stripes of gold, green and scarlet on the floor and stippling the walls. I got up and drew the blinds. I felt better then for some reason. I put the spent match-stalk in the earthenware tray on my desk and blew a spiral of blue smoke toward the cracks in the ceiling.

The noise of traffic came up muted and far away from the distant boulevard; almost at the edge of conscious hearing there followed the insistent sound of an ambulance siren. It was like the savage voice of the city; raw, ruthless and inhuman. Thank you, Emily Dickinson, I told myself. I sat back in my swivel chair and totted up a few points in what was left of my mind. Not that they amounted to much. Mrs Van Gimpel's assignment was setting something of a record, even for me. What I didn't know would have filled a stack of notebooks reaching from floor to ceiling.

Stella had left a late edition of the *Examiner* on my blotter; I didn't bother to go through it because she'd inked NOTHING in the top right-hand corner; that meant Ross still hadn't been found. Or at any rate that the police hadn't given out anything to the press about it. Though his body may not yet have been discovered; L.A. is a vast, impersonal place where people tend to mind their own business. There were cases on record where corpses had sat around for weeks waiting to be discovered.

I got out the two stapled photo-copy sheets Ross had given me a short while before he died. I ran down the long lists of names in the heavy silence of the office. Like he'd said Allied Zinc headed them up, with the name of Abraham Keefer in brackets. That was the persona Tombes had taken. I'd no doubt that other companies there were also Adams-operated if his organisation was laundering money and milking cash from the San Rosario operations.

But if Ross hadn't been part of the conspiracy and my conversation with him tended toward that theory, how else had Adams got an in to the set-up; let alone such an easy and apparently profitable operation. Some ideas which had been stirring in the primeval recesses of my mind started their round again.

I had the desk lamp on and I could see by the slats in the blinds that it was quite dark outside now. I got up and put the room light on too. It was time I was making tracks. I had a bottle of bourbon in the deep drawer of my desk but I didn't want to start on that trail. The bourbon was for the occasional evening snort when I might have a special visitor. I hadn't reached the solitary drinking stage; not yet, that is. Give it another ten years, Faraday, I told myself.

I was just sitting back at the desk, shuffling my thoughts around uselessly, when the phone rang. I picked it up, expecting Stella. I couldn't place the voice at first. Then I recognised it as Joseph's. He sounded agitated.

'Mr Faraday? I need your help.'

'Sure,' I said. 'Whatever I can do.'

'It's Mrs Van Gimpel,' he said. 'She phoned up from L.A., where she'd gone to see some friends. She'd tried to get hold of you but there was no reply to her call.'

'I've been here half an hour,' I said.'

'She phoned about then,' Joseph went on. 'I've been searching the estate since, in case the girls had come back.'

'It would help if you'd tell me what happened,' I said.

'Sorry, Mr Faraday,' Joseph mumbled. 'Mrs Van Gimpel sounded so upset. I've never known her like that. Apparently she and Miss Valerie had a terrible row over her friendship with Mr Adams. She went off to Adams' house in a dreadful rage. Mrs Van Gimpel seemed to think something awful might happen. Like her running off with him.'

I squinted wryly at the ceiling.

'That doesn't sound very terrible to me.'

'You didn't hear Mrs Van Gimpel, Mr Faraday,' Joseph said earnestly. 'She was almost hysterical. She's got a great love for her daughters. She said you were unobtainable so I was looking for Miss Erica to ask her help and advice. But she's not on the estate either.'

'You know Mark Adams' place and how to

160

get there?' I said.

'Sure, Mr Faraday. I got it marked on my large-scale. I figured I might have need of it one day. What do you want me to do?'

'Follow me up there,' I said. 'I might have need of you and you did volunteer.'

I could hear the satisfaction in the big butler's voice.

'Sure thing, Mr Faraday. You want me to bring a gun?'

'It might be an idea,' I said drily. 'There could be some unpleasant characters around. I'm a lot nearer to Adams' place than you are and if I leave now I should get there half an hour before you. But we'll have surprise at least.'

'Sure thing, Mr Faraday.'

There was hesitation in the voice now.

'I wouldn't have bothered you but I'm convinced there's going to be trouble. Adams wouldn't harm Valerie; he's too fond of her for that. But the people round him fear her influence with Mark Adams. They wouldn't scruple to get rid of her if it suited them. She knows that. She's wild and undisciplined, like I said. And she took a pistol with her, Mrs Van Gimpel says.'

'All right, Joseph,' I said. 'I got the picture now. Follow on up as soon as you can. And thanks.'

'Thank you, sir,' Joseph said.

He put the phone down. I reached over to

the desk drawer and got the bourbon bottle. I poured myself a stiff snort in one of the paper cups I fetched from the water cooler. It might be cold up in the hills tonight I told myself. You're a big liar, Faraday, I added.

I checked out the Smith-Wesson, made sure I had a fresh clip of cartridges in the holster. Then I phoned Stella, found her home and told her what I was doing and where I was going. Within three minutes I was on my way.

2

It was still raining but not so badly as before and I only had to use the wipers occasionally to filter out the fine mist which was forming as I drove out to Adams' place. I'd memorised the drive back in from last time and it was only a question of reversing the route on the large-scale I had pinned to the dashboard. I wore my lightweight raincoat in case the weather worsened and had the side window wound down to get the benefit of the air.

The traffic was fairly thin this time of the evening and I hit the section I wanted in under the half hour and turned the Buick's bonnet up into the foothills. A number of ideas were crystallising now but I had nothing that would stand up anywhere, either legally or as a coherent narrative. Like I'd told Joseph I'd play it by ear. But if Valerie Van Gimpel had gone berserk over Adams and taken a gun up there anything might happen. The whole case could fall apart. And if so I'd like to be there to see if I could make any sense of the pieces.

The rain was a little heavier now and I'd got the wipers on permanently. I was having some difficulty in making out the intersections and I slackened speed a little, looking vainly through the cleared segment of windshield for any distinguishing landscape features. The girl would have arrived at the estate long ago and anything could have happened by now. But I'd promised Joseph and through him, Mrs Van Gimpel, and I had to try.

The Smith-Wesson made a reassuring pressure against my chest muscles as I tooled the Buick over on to the lane I wanted; it was almost like the last time I'd been up here. Just a flash of white fencing and then the black tarmac of the private roadway, now blurred and distorted with the rain. I was trying to recall exactly how long the drive was; and some of its distinctive features.

The wind was gusting heavily and I could see, by my lowered mainbeams, that the tops of the trees that fringed the drive were whipping and bending over. I had the wind direction now; it was blowing away from the house. That was a help at least because it meant the noise of the motor wouldn't be heard up there. Certainly at this distance because I was still a long way off.

I decided to press on in low gear and on side-lights only which would give me a chance of getting close; otherwise I would have a long walk in addition to getting drowned. But time, not discomfort, was the most important thing if I was to save Valerie Van Gimpel from the consequences of her own folly. I cast a glance at my watch; with a little luck Joseph should show within half an hour. And that would even the odds up a little.

I was having great difficulty seeing the edges of the drive. There was no moon and the blackness of the tarmac surface of the private road didn't help; there was nothing but dark shadow and I slowed to a crawl. I had almost given up when I saw a faint light in the sky ahead, way above the tree tops. I pulled the Buick as far into my near-side edge as I could and killed the motor. I transferred the Smith-Wesson into my raincoat pocket and got out the passenger door, the rain cold and stinging against my face.

Nothing could have been a greater contrast to my first visit; the heaviness of the rain; the comparative darkness of the house; and the sodden undergrowth thrashing in the night wind. I gritted my way cautiously across the concourse. There were no other vehicles around that I could see and I figured they'd probably gone via the curving driveway that led to the main entrance, in view of the weather.

I was up on top of the steps now and could see there were only a few lights showing in the vast facade. I went down the paved walk beneath the pergola, the perfume of tropical plants freshened and accentuated by the rain. The butt of the Smith-Wesson was chill against my finger-tips and I eased off on to the grass as I got closer to the huge white Christmas-cake building.

There were two or three lights piercing the upper storeys; probably from bedrooms or public rooms on the third floor; and not more than three or four on the ground floor. It was difficult to make out because of the architectural features of the house and the intervening shrubbery.

I was getting nice and wet now but I was still pretty cautious; I was watching where I put my feet and keeping my eyes peeled for any shadows moving across the ground floor windows. I didn't see anything but that didn't mean there wasn't anyone around. I got the Smith-Wesson out my pocket and held it, barrel down, beneath my inverted palm, sheltering it from the rain.

I was only about ten yards away from the front of the house now and I stopped in the shadow of the trellis-work to take stock of my position. The room where the dance had been held was dark and silent. I walked on in the open, across the lawn, making for the conservatory entrance. A light burned dimly inside, like there was someone in the glasshouses and if I remembered the geography correctly there was a pillared arcade where I could at least shelter from the rain.

I heard and saw nothing but I could feel my heart pumping in my throat as I ran across the open space to the shadowy shelter of the colonnade. It wasn't only the exercise either. The evening could end up disastrously unless I made the right decision. I checked my watch again; there was no sense in making my move until I was sure Joseph would show within a short while. On the other hand I had Valerie Van Gimpel to consider. Like always they were finely balanced considerations.

I worked along beneath the elegant white roof, past the gleaming white pillars of the arcade, glad to be out of the rain. I checked the Smith-Wesson, spun the chambers. The minute snick the action made stopped me in my tracks for a split-second.

There were the double glass doors through which I'd come in with Tombes originally. I glanced back behind me; my eyes were used to the shadows now but I couldn't see anyone in rear. There was no reason why there should have been and no-one knew I was coming here. No-one, that is, except for Joseph and Mrs Van Gimpel. I stopped again, the tumblers of my mind beginning to turn. I was close to the glass doors. One of them was ajar, like someone had recently passed through and the door had eased back, without closing.

I got up close and peered through. There was no-one in the lobby; nothing but the light from the antique brass lantern throwing its illumination down blandly on the black and white tiled marble floor; and gleaming on the few pieces of furniture. The blue and gold of the rafters made a sumptuous, almost cathedral-like atmosphere in here. That was about the only religious thing at Adams' place.

I stayed in the darkness of the arcade for perhaps another three seconds; I could neither see nor hear anything unusual but I knew if I hung about any longer my nerve would begin to crack. I pushed the door; it gave and opened slightly. I could see all the interior of the lobby now. It was empty of everything except for California climate.

There were lights burning dimly, far off, among the dark fronds and fleshy-looking plants of the glass-house; I got inside the lobby quickly, glancing back down the arcade. Nothing moved in all the long façade and the only sound in here was the low, insistent beat of the clock in its polished case up against the far wall.

I went over quickly to stand in the shadow of the polished mahogany looking down to the steaming, moist panes of the conservatory behind. It was difficult to make out anything except for the motionless shapes of plant-life; it was certain I could see nothing within. Not equally certain that anyone inside couldn't see out. It was a chance I couldn't afford to take.

Besides, it left out of account the business room in which Adams had first received me. If I went on down the conservatory that would leave the door in rear; I didn't know what was in there. I had to find out first. I thought I was safe enough for the moment; I remembered Tombes had let himself into a sort of double lobby within the glass-house. That was all steamed up too; and the shrubbery and plants blocked the main glass wall which arched to the ceiling.

I walked over toward the business room door, my nerves beginning to crawl slightly, a pulse beating in my throat. The Smith-Wesson suddenly felt very heavy in my hand, the barrel dragging the weapon downward toward the floor. A thin bead of sweat ran down my forehead to mingle with the cold moisture of the rain on my face. I put my ear against the panel.

There was a dull, blank silence from the room beyond. I got hold of the brass handle. It turned gently and easily with the smooth precision of well-oiled mechanism. The piece was probably a genuine eighteenth century door; brought from England possibly; the lock made by a long-dead master craftsman. You're getting poetic again, Mike, I told myself.

I had the door open now. It came away soundlessly; an inch, two inches. I could see into the room; the lights burned against the panelled walls, gleamed on the gilded spines of the books on the shelves; and on the strange desk with the green baize surface. The place was empty all right. I pulled the door all the way open and stepped into the room.

That was when the fat man came up from behind the desk. He still wore the white raincoat, streaked and dappled with rain; and the light glinted on the kindly eyes beneath the thick glasses. Something silvery and glittering split the air between us as I brought the Smith-Wesson barrel up.

CHAPTER NINETEEN

1

I felt a pain in my ear. The silver streak resolved itself into the fat man's knife which stuck quivering in the door-jamb. I was on my knees now. The Smith-Wesson seemed to make a very loud detonation in the silence of Adams' business room. The fat man staggered, dimly seen through the cloud of blue smoke. He had the big pistol halfway out the pocket of his raincoat but its barrel was already dipped toward the floor as the slug punched him away.

He hit the elegant panelling on the far wall with a jagged splintering sound and slid downward, scarlet spreading on the front of his raincoat. His cannon detonated as it hit the floor and I flinched at the explosion, the slug tearing a big hole in the ceiling. Plaster rained downward like flour, making an eerie white mist.

I was trembling a little as I got up and went over to Lester. His eyes were wide open behind the glasses. They looked incredulous. His fat body trembled once or twice and a big tear ran down from his right eyelid to the corner of his mouth. A bubbling froth oozed from his lips; he shook himself once or twice like a dog after a swim and then found he was dead.

It seemed incredibly quiet in the room. I put the Smith-Wesson down on the desk with the green baize top.

'That's right, Mr Faraday,' said a soft voice.

I turned very slowly, a mass of snakes squirming at the base of my spine. Eli Tombes looked very big and very deadly as he stepped out from behind one of the big bookcases at the far corner of the room. He still wore the check suit and his silver hair glistened beneath the lamps above his graveyard smile.

'We figured you might be along this evening.'

He exposed his square teeth again in a thin smile and motioned with the snout of the blued steel automatic he held in his fist. He looked down at the body of the fat man.

Smoke was still ascending slowly to the ceiling.

'A pity,' he said slowly. 'Lester was a good operator but a fool. I told him a knife could never beat a gun.'

He looked at me quickly, made an imperative gesture with the barrel of the automatic.

'Get away from the desk, Mr Faraday.'

I did like he said. There was no profit in trying anything else. I felt something warm on my neck then, put up my hand. It came away scarlet. Tombes swivelled the barrel again as I put my hand in my pocket, brought out my handkerchief. I staunched the bleeding of the lobe of my ear where the fat man's knife had nicked it. I looked at the long, thin blade in the door-jamb. It had been thrown so hard it had sunk in about two inches.

'Won't the servants be along in a minute?' I said.

Tombes looked at me mockingly.

'They sleep the other side of the house,' he said. 'They don't come into this wing at night in any case.'

He bared his teeth again.

'We have things going on here. They know better than to intrude.'

'That must be very convenient,' I said.

Tombes walked over casually and sat down on top of the desk to face me. He scooped up the Smith-Wesson and put it in his pocket.

'It is, Mr Faraday,' he said evenly.

I went over and sat down in one of Adams' big leather chairs. Tombes sat and watched me without saying anything.

'You mind if I smoke?' I said.

He shrugged.

'It won't make much difference now.'

He watched me from beneath half-closed lids as I lit up. I spun the used match-stalk over on to the polished parquet floor near his chair. His smile widened a little but he didn't shift his position.

'Won't Mr Adams be annoyed at all the mess in here?' I said.

He shook his head.

'Mr Adams won't need to know anything about it. I'll lock this up and get things discreetly repaired.'

'You'll find Mr Lester a little more difficult to get rid of.'

Tombes shook his head, the smile still lingering.

'I think not. We have efficient garbage disposal methods.'

I blew out a column of smoke toward the ceiling, conscious that the open door of the room was at an angle to Tombes. From where I sat I could see the lobby.

'Where is Mr Adams?' I said.

Tombes shook his head slowly.

'He's otherwise engaged,' he said.

He glanced over toward the door but he obviously couldn't see anything.

'In the conservatory. Or busy with even more worthwhile pursuits.'

He drew himself up, seeming to exude power and strength. The big automatic never wavered as he held it sighted steadily on my gut.

'You can't hear anything here, Mr Faraday. This part of the house was designed specifically and purpose-built.'

He glanced at his wrist-watch. I wondered if he was waiting for the wheel-man in the black sedan. I interrupted quickly.

'You mind if we talk for a while? There's a few things I'd like to get straight in my mind.'

Tombes held out his hands in an expansive gesture.

'Why not?' he told the ceiling. 'After all, you'll be dead within half an hour.'

'Why?' I said.

Tombes spread his hands wide again.

'Why what?'

'Mrs Van Gimpel hired me to keep an eye on her youngest daughter,' I said. 'A couple of conversations later people start getting killed. Someone takes three shots at me. I'd like to know why. Just for the record.'

Tombes' hard mouth was set in a thin, straight line. He rubbed his jaw with his unoccupied hand, keeping the gun barrel steady. He was still sitting on the desk and I was mentally measuring the distance between us. It was too far.

'You're talking about Ross?'

I nodded.

Tombes shifted on the surface of the desk and shrugged.

'I haven't got all the answers. That's the truth. I can only say what's within my own purview.'

He glanced over at the body of the fat man.

'Lester was always impulsive. He consistently exceeded instructions. He followed you the night you were up here. He was supposed to make sure you didn't get too close to the truth. Those were my orders.'

He made a grimace, his eyes down on the floor now, like he was picking his words with care.

'He listens at the window, decides Ross is getting too gabby. So he kills him.'

He gave a bleak, humourless smile.

'An inoffensive, innocent guy and my major contact with San Rosario. A man who'll be difficult to replace. A foul-up of the first water. I can't say I'm sorry you took Lester out, Mr Faraday.'

I tapped the ash off my cigarette on my shoe. The movement, slight as it was, brought up the big man's cannon.

'What truth was I supposed to be getting close to?' I said.

Tombes narrowed his eyes to slits.

'That's the major one, Mr Faraday. And still restricted information. You'll have to carry that unanswered question to the Big Wheel in the Sky.'

'I didn't know you were so poetic,' I said.

Tombes shook his head, his fashionably cut silver hair shining under the lamps.

'I am a man of many parts, Mr Faraday.'

'And you didn't order me taken out?' I said.

Tombes shook his head, his eyes genuinely puzzled.

'For what it's worth, no. But now it's different. You've taken yourself out.'

'It won't stop there,' I said. 'Mrs Van Gimpel will never agree to Adams marrying her daughter. She'll spend millions of dollars to stop it. There'll be other people after me. And maybe they'll dig deeper into Adams' activities.'

Tombes scratched his jaw again. His expression didn't change a fraction.

'I'm sure that's true, Mr Faraday. And I'm not convinced Mr Adams is right to take it so lightly. But it's not your problem. It's mine and Mr Adams. Now, if you're all through . . .'

'Not quite,' I said. 'There are a number of pieces I haven't got. Things that don't fit. Mrs Van Gimpel is a millionairess. Adams is a millionaire. Their interests shouldn't conflict. Combined, their assets should be unbeatable. That is, if you don't mind where your money comes from.'

Tombes looked at me mockingly.

'That's the crux of the problem, Mr

175

Faraday,' he said softly. 'You can't break it without the key. Ross was unwittingly part of it and you made Lester take him out. Someone has to pay for it. He's left a big hole in the organisation.'

My brain was clicking over like the works of a fruit-machine paying out a big jackpot now. Tombes was throwing me nuggets of information but a major cog was missing in there; causing the wheels to go round without the ratchets engaging the flywheel. Or something about that price-range.

For the first time I could hear the faint ticking of the big cased clock outside in the lobby. It may have been my imagination but I fancied I could hear a distant fretting noise too, whose provenance escaped me. I glanced quickly at Tombes but he obviously hadn't heard anything. But then he was a lot farther from the door than I was.

'Can we do a deal?' I said.

Tombes shook his head, his mouth a mathematically straight line beneath his massive nose. 'No deals, Faraday,' he said.

He relaxed the barrel of the pistol slightly. 'You're a pro, like me. You just got to take the breaks as they fall.'

'That's right,' I said.

Tombes stood up. He looked gigantic in his natty suiting as he raised the pistol.

'No sense in hanging around, Mr Faraday. It isn't fair on you.'

176

'Nice of you to think about that aspect,' I said.

I got up too. My heart was thumping in my chest and my throat felt strained and dry. The pistol barrel looked as big as a cargo hangar at L.A. International as it came up toward me. The click as the safety went off sounded like the ceiling was coming in.

I glanced around, I was too far in line with the door.

'Can I say something?'

Tombes shook his head.

'It won't make any difference, man. Make it snappy.'

The pistol barrel moved aside for a fraction. I had my hand under the carved arm of the big leather chair. I slid it along the parquet with all my strength. Tombes looked taken aback. He moved agilely aside and it crashed into the desk. I moved over while he was doing that. He had the gun up again now.

'That was really silly, Mr Faraday,' he said.

I still held the handkerchief to my ear and now I took it down. The bleeding had stopped.

'It doesn't change anything,' Tombes continued.

I shook my head.

'It might make all the difference between you shooting me now or not at all,' I said.

Tombes brought the pistol up. His mocking smile was the last thing I saw as the whole room erupted into smoke and flame.

CHAPTER TWENTY

1

I was on the floor, conscious that Tombes'
bullet had gone into one of the bookcases.
Glass shattered and Tombes was cartwheeling
over the desk. His face expressed shock and
surprise. He hit the fireplace and keeled over,
taking a lot of vases and fancy ornaments with
him. The noise must have reached to L.A. and
back and yet the silence which followed had an
ear-aching quality. There was no sound of
running feet; cries of alarm; or shouts from the
servants.

Joseph's bronze face looked round the door
cautiously, smoke still coming from the muzzle
of his big cannon. He looked over at the
crumpled figures of the fat man and Tombes.
The latter's suit was all peppered with holes.
He must have put at least four slugs into him. I
started getting up, found I was trembling.

'You took your time,' I said.

'But I got here,' Joseph said.

He looked down admiringly at the
punctured figure of Tombes.

'Like I said, I could take the fuzz off a
peach,' he said.

'We weren't dealing with peaches,' I said.

Joseph's face seemed to dissolve then. He

178

crumpled and I saw scarlet stains spreading out on the front of his immaculate suit. I hadn't noticed it before because he was standing side on to me.

I got to him quickly, helped him to a chair. I took his handkerchief and formed a pad which I made him hold over the wound. I took his pistol and went out into the lobby. There was nothing but silence and order there under the soft glare of the ceiling lantern. I went over and locked the big glass entrance doors just in case the hood in the black sedan showed.

I went back to Joseph, poured him a stiff brandy from Adams' stock. I took it over and the big man gulped it down like it was water. Some of the greyness disappeared from his face.

'Bad?' I said.

He shook his head.

'Painful. I was lucky. But it may have grazed the bone.'

I went over to Tombes, being careful where I put my feet. I took the Smith-Wesson and replaced it in my shoulder-holster. I felt properly dressed then. I went across to Joseph and poured him another shot. I gave him his pistol back.

'You think you can handle things here for a few minutes. I've got to go see the master of the house.'

Joseph nodded, his face distorted with pain.

'Sure. Just so it's not too long. I'd like to get

some medical attention soon. You want me to ring the police?'

I shook my head.

'Not yet. The night isn't over and I want to try and wind this up before the boys in blue get here.'

Joseph nodded, putting the glass to his mouth again. The place looked like the last act of Macbeth as I went on out. I was warm now in my raincoat and I took it off and put it down on the bench in the hall. The door to the conservatory lobby was covered with steam and the heat hit me like a wall as I went on in.

I walked through for perhaps ten yards and then opened the far door, glancing back as I did so. I'd been right. Nothing of the lobby could be seen from here and the two sets of doors, to say nothing of the walls of Adams' business room would have damped down the shots like they'd never existed. I went on through the second lobby door. The heat really did hit me then.

The place was fantastically beautiful with the steam; the delicate brilliance of the blooms; and the sound of running water, but I had no time for the W. H. Hudson stuff tonight. I went on down, holding the Smith-Wesson inconspicuously at my side, walking on the balls of my feet.

2

Adams, dressed like before in white open-neck shirt and silver-grey trousers, had his back to me. He was standing up the far end of the vast structure, backgrounded by the polished waxiness of fleshy leaves; busying himself with a pipette and a glass beaker. He was so absorbed that he almost started at the scrape of my shoe on the tiling behind him. I had to admire his self-control, though.

'Mr Faraday!'

His smile was genuine and unforced.

'What brings you here this evening, uninvited and unannounced?'

'Business,' I said.

He put the pipette and the beaker down on a bench very deliberately and wiped his hand on a sheet of tissues he took from a box at his side. He seemed supremely at ease. I liked his style but this was no time for the social niceties. I glanced round the conservatory; there was another door at the far end, which evidently led back to the house.

That was the only thing I could see; the rest of the wall area and the paths beyond were masked by the mass of greenery which reared some thirty or forty feet above our heads.

Adams went in for a good deal of stuff beside orchids; I'd never asked him what these things were called. There probably wouldn't be an opportunity now.

'There's been some trouble,' I said. 'I came out here to see Valerie Van Gimpel and take her back home. Her mother was worried about her.'

Adams' film-star image seemed a little dented now. Even the brilliant blond hair; the even teeth and the open, tanned face appeared somehow tarnished. Maybe it was just the steamy atmosphere in here. Already, my shirt was like crumpled paper round my neck.

Adams gave me one of his ready smiles.

'I can assure you she isn't here, Mr Faraday. You're welcome to search the place. She rang me earlier this evening. She was staying with her mother at some friends' apartment in L.A. I have the number if you wish to check.'

I shook my head.

'That won't be necessary. We have more serious things to attend to.'

Adams' smile widened. Then he glanced down at my side and laughed out loud.

'Oh, come, Mr Faraday! There's no need to be melodramatic. You won't need that pistol.'

I shook my head.

'You still don't understand, Mr Adams. Two of your boys tried to kill me just now. They're lying dead back in your business room. I wouldn't be here now if it hadn't been for Mrs Van Gimpel's butler.'

Adams had an incredulous expression on his

face. He rocked back on his heels a few times.

'It's a preposterous story, Mr Faraday!'

'You have only to step through to ascertain its truth,' I said.

Adams cast a quick glance back over his shoulder at the far door. He looked distinctly uneasy and off balance at that moment.

'I'd rather not do that, Mr Faraday. I'll take your word for it.'

I didn't answer him. There was white metal ornamental scrollwork all over the place. I walked across to one of the iron central pillars where Adams' coat and tie were hanging. I went through his jacket pockets. The big man looked amused.

'I don't carry firearms, Mr Faraday. That's your prerogative. I don't need them in my line of business.'

'You may have to do your own dirty work from now on,' I said.

He looked at me sharply.

'Meaning what? And you didn't tell me the names of those people apparently lying dead in my house.'

I traded glances with him.

'Your fat friend for one,' I told him. 'Eli Tombes for the other. Or Mr Keefer if you prefer. That will do for starters. Like I said, they tried to kill me.'

Mark Adams passed his tongue across his lips like his mouth had suddenly gone dry.

'Well, well. This does call for some thought,

Mr Faraday.'

'I'm glad you agree,' I said.

His eyes were steady and unwavering again. Once more I noticed their strange violet quality.

'You've called the police?'

'Not yet,' I said. 'I thought it best to see you first. And we ought to get Joseph to hospital right away. He stopped one of Tombes' slugs in the shoulder.'

Adams was again the professional wheeler-dealer.

'What would be your price to forget about this?'

I looked at him incredulously.

'I already told you, Mr Adams. No deals.'

He smiled ruefully, like he'd been bested at cards. He certainly had great style.

'Oh, well, Mr Faraday, I think I can handle this mess, given a few hours. Two bodies shouldn't present an insuperable problem.'

I stared at him for a long moment.

'Waste disposal unit, I suppose?'

He shook his head mockingly.

'Nothing so crude, Mr Faraday. I could perhaps get my gardeners to clear up the rubbish in the morning.'

I grinned.

'If you had time.'

'Meaning you might give me time?'

I walked a yard or two off and put the Smith-Wesson back in my holster.

'Possibly. We might do a trade-off. I have my client and the girl to think of. They must be kept out of this.'

Adams gave me another of his mocking smiles. Sweat was beginning to trickle down from the corners of his eyes into the V of his shirt now.

'The price being my withdrawal from the family matrimonial stakes.'

'Something like that,' I said.

Adams drew himself up.

'No deal. Let me tell you something, Mr Faraday. I built up and I own that family. Nothing will stop me. Not you, nor Mrs Van Gimpel and not even a houseful of corpses.'

'I'm not sure I follow,' I said.

Adams shook his head angrily. He was slightly crouched now, as though he'd heard a door close somewhere in the house.

'Let me spell it out for you, seeing that we are talking in confidence. Valerie is in love with me. She's nineteen and beautiful. With her I could control the whole of San Rosario. It's a great patrimony.'

'Aren't you forgetting the old lady?' I said. 'To say nothing of Erica? She's a lawyer and is due to take over.'

Adams shook his head impatiently.

'You still don't understand, Mr Faraday. I run both girls. Erica belongs to me too. She would be better for me, undoubtedly, with her fine mind and legal training. But a girl of

185

nineteen is malleable and easily controlled. Valerie would do anything for me.'

'But you don't love her?' I said.

Adams smiled faintly.

'I've never loved anyone in my life but myself, Mr Faraday.'

'And that's your last word?' I said.

Adams shrugged.

'That's my last word.'

I turned as there came a light footstep on the tiling. That was when the tall blonde with the tangled mane of hair, her face white and set, madness staring in her eyes, stepped out of the greenness of that tropical jungle and shot Adams at point-blank range through the chest.

CHAPTER TWENTY-ONE

1

'It's a great way to finish the evening,' I said.

I took the pistol from her. Erica Van Gimpel's eyes were wide and crazy and spittle made little flecks of foam on her lips. She was naked except for the high-heel shoes and the white towelling bathrobe which hung open from her shoulders. I went over to Adams. All the front of his shirt was scorched and the flesh charred, the muzzle-flash had been so close. He was already dead. There was nothing anyone could do.

I closed up the girl's dressing gown, tied it with the cord and slapped her a couple of times round the face. She suddenly crumpled and burst into a fit of sobbing. She would have thrown herself on Adams' body if I hadn't stopped her.

'You did a fine job,' I said. 'Your mother would be proud of you. But it calls for some thought.'

I took her up the far end of the conservatory and told her to stay put, sitting her on one of the wrought iron chairs I found there. I went quickly back down the glasshouse; I wiped off the automatic, had a second thought then. I went back to the girl.

'Is the pistol yours?'

She shook her head dully.

'He was foul, Mr Faraday. He promised to marry me.'

'He made a lot of promises,' I said. 'Is the pistol yours?'

She shook her head.

'It belongs to Mark. I took it from the bureau in the bedroom.'

'Why?' I said. 'And why did you follow him down here tonight?'

The girl's mouth was closed tight now and she was beginning to tremble. Soon she would be in shock.

'I guessed what he intended to do. I could sense he was getting tired of me. We had a row

187

earlier tonight. I took the pistol and searched the house for him. I only intended to frighten him into agreeing to our marriage. Then I heard what he was saying about me and Valerie and something snapped.'

'It figures,' I said. 'It seems to run in the family.'

I picked her up by the shoulders and ran her up the glasshouse toward the far door.

'Go collect your things and get dressed,' I said. 'Make sure no-one sees you. And if he has any of your letters, bring those too. This place will be swarming with law in a couple of hours.'

The girl nodded, shook her head once or twice like she was coming out of a bad dream. She went off, closing the door behind her. I went back to Adams, pressed the gun into the stiffening fingers of his right hand, close to the wound, trying to make it as natural as possible.

Then I went quickly to Joseph. He was still doubled up in pain but said he could hold out. I filled him in in a few sentences and returned to the conservatory. It was cooler outside but I had to make sure the girl didn't do anything silly. So I waited until she came. It was only ten minutes but it seemed like ten hours. She had on a white summer outfit and she looked as wide-eyed and innocent as a Cole Porter musical.

'You got everything?'
She nodded.

'I made sure, Mr Faraday. Are we going to the police?'

I shook my head.

'You're in the clear if you keep your mouth shut. And don't go messing around out of your depth in future.'

She put her face forward and came into my arms. I pushed her away, none too gently.

'Save it for the right man,' I said.

We went on back, closing the conservatory door behind us. In the lobby the air seemed to strike cold and chill. I put my raincoat on, went to collect Joseph. The girl got the other side and we held him beneath the shoulders.

The whole house seemed lapped in an unearthly and ghostly silence like something out of the Sleeping Beauty. I locked the business room door and pocketed the key. When we reached the bottom of the steps the girl got behind the wheel of the heap Joseph had come in, with the butler beside her. I told her to follow me in and went back to the Buick, treading between the puddles beneath the lashing rain.

We pulled out in the darkness and the rain, heading for the hospital and the boys in blue, Adams' fancy Christmas cake dream fading in the misty night behind us.

2

'So how do you read the tangle?' Stella said drily.

She went through Mrs Van Gimpel's letter again with a frown. Then she straightened up the cheque for the third time and stared at the amount incredulously.

'Ten thousand, Mike! Are you keeping it?'

'Too true I'm keeping it,' I said. 'I earned it.'

I looked at her grimly.

'It's her way of paying me off.'

Stella made a little clicking noise with her teeth. Today she wore a pale blue silk dress that set her figure off in a way there should be legislation against and the gold bell of her hair sparkled and shimmered in the bright sunlight which threw heavy bands of black and yellow across the floor of the office.

'I don't understand that, either. And why should she have left for a cruise to Europe with the girls? It doesn't make sense. Surely she could have stayed to thank you.'

'That wasn't on the cards,' I said. 'The money was her way of thanking me. It's what the rich always do.'

I stared up at the cracks in the ceiling.

'She fled would be the proper way to put it.'

Stella got up with a swift, rippling

movement. She went over to switch the coffee percolator on.

'Did you get those books for Joseph?' I said. 'He finds it boring in the hospital.'

'Certainly,' Stella said, putting her head round the ground-glass screen. 'We'll both go when we shut up shop. Besides, he's only there for another three days.'

'Joseph's an intellectual,' I said. 'He'll go crazy without something brilliant and stimulating to read.'

Stella came back from the alcove and sat on a corner of my desk, smiling.

'The police will want to see you again, Mike.'

'It's all fixed up for Monday,' I said. 'They're still puzzled but I'm in the clear.'

'They're not the only ones,' Stella said.

I took the hint.

'Mrs Van Gimpel wanted to get rid of Adams,' I said. 'It's as simple as that.'

'You knew that when you took the case,' Stella said, putting the coffee down on my blotter.

I shook my head.

'You're reading it the wrong way round, honey. Let's go back to the beginning.'

Stella's eyes were wide and serious.

'From when Max Van Gimpel fell off the bridge?'

I nodded.

'Exactly. But some people said he was

191

pushed. By a big man. My guess is a professional killer.'

Stella put her spoon down with a little chinking noise in the silence.

'Eli Tombes?'

'That's the way I read it. You were right. Adams didn't care a cent for my probing. I had nothing on him and couldn't do anything to him and he knew it. But he was concerned about his relationship with the girls. He didn't want me spoiling it. So, in a very polite way, he warned me off.'

I set fire to another cigarette, the rasp of the match-head against the box an intrusion in the silence.

'Tombes was a different proposition. He had something to lose. And he didn't want me nosing around in the Max Van Gimpel murder. So he sent the fat man to keep tabs on me. He exceeded his instructions and took out Ross, instead of me.'

Stella shivered suddenly, like it had grown cold in here.

'You can't prove any of this, Mike.'

'It doesn't matter now,' I said. 'The case is finished. And Tombes and the fat boy got dead anyway. There'll be no charges against me or Joseph. I had that from the Chief himself.'

Stella looked at me dubiously.

'There are still a lot of loose ends.'

'Sure,' I said. 'And all of this is conjecture. That's why Mrs Van Gimpel went away. She'd succeeded in her objective. She'd gotten rid of the one man she feared, Mark Adams. And the threat to her empire with his marriage to her daughter had been removed. She relied on me to achieve that for her. But the way I told the story, Adams' fake suicide stands up. So she still wins.'

Stella put up a pink-nailed hand to her immaculate coiffure.

'And I still don't understand, Mike.'

'You're not yourself today, honey,' I said. 'I'm speaking your lines. Usually, you spell it out and I listen.'

Stella gave me a lazy smile that I could have watched all afternoon.

'The police more or less bought my story,' I said. 'Adams was trying to muscle in on the San Rosario Corporation. They killed Ross because he refused their pressuring; they couldn't corrupt him. I owed him that much. Adams was behind the whole thing; after the shoot-out, I confronted him. As I went out to call the police he put a bullet through his heart.'

I spread my hands on the blotter.

'Open and shut. A few holes here and there, if you examine it more closely, but the police were forced to buy it.'

'Adams wouldn't have killed himself in a million years, Mike,' Stella said.

'Of course not,' I said. 'But it's good enough for the public. And the police, while they might have their suspicions, have to go along with it now. All nice and neat.'

There was silence between us for a moment or two. I watched my cigarette smoke drifting up toward the ceiling.

'Which brings us full circle. Back to Mrs Van Gimpel. She needed someone like me. A private eye with a heart of gold, steel-like muscles and a sense of integrity that stretches from here to San Francisco.'

Stella grinned.

'Save it for your business cards.'

'I'll take it under advisement,' I said. 'Max Van Gimpel was murdered. Taken out by Tombes, like I said. He was given instructions by Adams. Who in turn was given the commission by Gimpel's wife.'

Stella's face was a picture.

'This is all theorising, Mike . . .'

'Of course,' I said. 'But it's the only thing that fits. Van Gimpel dives off the bridge. After a suitable period of mourning Mrs Van Gimpel picks up eight million dollars. She founds the San Rosario Corporation and makes a hundred times that. But all the while she has Adams, the only man who knows her secret, on her neck. Perhaps she met him socially at one time; who knows. He took the job on for a price; she had to have professional help in that area. You know what the price was.'

Stella nodded slowly.

'A slice of San Rosario.'

'That had to be it,' I said. 'Millionaires always want more. Adams was no exception.'

'Allied Zinc and the other companies were quite genuine. The profits went to Adams. The police have already discovered that many of the set-ups on Ross' list are genuine businesses, registered with San Rosario, and legitimately using their computer time. I've no doubt that Adams was laundering a lot of dirty money there as well, but basically the thing was fool-proof.'

'Until Adams decided to become too greedy?' Stella said.

I knocked off the ash from my cigarette in the earthenware tray on my desk.

'Undoubtedly. Supposing he started to blackmail Mrs Van Gimpel for a bigger cut. The situation was becoming intolerable. Then he made it known that he wanted to marry her youngest daughter. Apart from knocking off Erica on the side. So she had to get rid of him.'

A frown passed over Stella's face.

'Accepting your somewhat crude version, Mike, I think you have it.'

I blew out another spiral of smoke.

'It was too much. Valerie never went berserk or drove up to Adams' place with a gun. She was with Mrs Van Gimpel staying with friends in L.A. I had that from Adams himself, who offered to give me the phone number; and I had no reason to doubt him. It

195

was Erica up there, which Mrs Van Gimpel didn't know about.'

'So she rang Joseph and gave him a dramatic story,' Stella said. 'Knowing you would go charging in and something lethal might happen.'

'That's about it,' I said. 'She couldn't be sure but she knew if she leaned on Adams hard enough through me something would crack in the end. She was probably relying on Tombes and the fat man. In the end, through Erica, the whole case fell apart by itself.'

'You've been kind to her,' Stella said softly.

I looked at her quickly.

'Over Erica. She was foolish but Adams was very plausible. I didn't want her to go to prison for twenty years. And Adams deserved to die anyway.'

'And Mrs Van Gimpel,' Stella said.

I shrugged.

'I can't prove anything. She'll just have to live with her conscience. Such as it is.'

'And a hundred million dollars,' Stella reminded me.

I was silent for a moment, thinking of Max Van Gimpel going off the bridge into the gorge all those years ago; of Valerie swimming at the pool; the apparent sincerity of Erica in the restaurant; of Mrs Van Gimpel's pain as she walked with her stick. What was the point of stirring things up any more; let them all live with their consciences. Such as they were.

There were other pictures too; the fat man drawing his knife in the garage; Tombes going down to death; Adams slumped in the glasshouse; Ross collapsing with the knife in his back. It was tough about Ross. He was the one innocent among all these people; but then the innocent always get caught in the crossfire.

'You haven't explained about those two bullets and the shots fired at you,' Stella said.

She got up to fetch me another cup of coffee.

'That wasn't too hard to figure once the light showed,' I said. 'At the thirteenth hour, of course.'

Stella came back with the coffee, giving me one of her mysterious smiles.

'Adams and Valerie had fallen out over the possible marriage. My hunch is that he couldn't make up his mind over the two girls. There were quarrels and bitter arguments. It was Valerie who fired at Adams down the drive of Spanish Oaks. The bullets missed and lodged in a tree. Like I said, by the calibre, it was more like a woman's weapon. It shook Adams and he decided to agree to the marriage. Certainly, when he went out the estate, the electronic scanner showed him as clean. He told me he never carried firearms.'

I leaned forward in my swivel chair and stubbed out my cigarette. It was very quiet in the office now and even the hum of the mid-afternoon traffic appeared to have died away.

'Adams thought he could control a nineteen-year-old girl much more easily than Erica. He may have been wrong. She was neurotic, volatile and unstable. She was probably due to meet Adams the night I went to the restaurant. Maybe Tombes was going to take her after he'd picked up the computer material from Ross. She saw me in the parking lot. She was obsessed with the dream of marrying Adams and being something more important than a secretary in her millionairess mother's business. Maybe she just wanted to warn me off. Or take me out to preserve her marriage plans. I've thought it over since the night Adams bought it and that's got to be the explanation.'

Stella looked at me in mock admiration. Then she shivered again.

'Nice people, Mike.'

I nodded, picking up the *Examiner* cuttings Stella was clipping for her files.

'The case came apart by itself, Mike,' she said.

'Adams seemed the nicest person in the whole business,' I said.

I sat back at my desk, riffling the material. I picked up one cutting, holding it sidewise.

'What the hell's this?' I said.

Stella smiled faintly.

'*The Orchid Fanciers' Gazette,*' she said.

I read out the intro of the cutting aloud.

'Last of the great orchid fanciers, Mark Adams died among the blossoms he loved.'

I stared across the desk at Stella.

'You'd have thought he died in bed the way they put it,' I said.

Stella gurgled to herself. When she came back from clearing the coffee cups she sat down in the client's chair and looked at me with very blue eyes, cupping her chin in her hands. I went on checking the cuttings.

'They should have put it under gardening notes,' I said.

Stella smiled.

'Nice people,' she said again.

I nodded.

'Tuxedo Park,' I said.

We hope you have enjoyed this Large Print book. Other Chivers Press or Thorndike Press Large Print books are available at your library or directly from the publishers.

For more information about current and forthcoming titles, please call or write, without obligation, to:

Chivers Large Print
published by BBC Audiobooks Ltd
St James House, The Square
Lower Bristol Road
Bath BA2 3BH
UK
email: bbcaudiobooks@bbc.co.uk
www.bbcaudiobooks.co.uk

OR

Thorndike Press
295 Kennedy Memorial Drive
Waterville
Maine 04901
USA
www.gale.com/thorndike
www.gale.com/wheeler

All our Large Print titles are designed for easy reading, and all our books are made to last.